3

SIMENON, GEORGES
WIDOWER

($10.95)

WAYNE PUBLIC LIBRARY
MAIN LIBRARY
475 Valley Road
Wayne, N. J. 07470

Books may be returned at any
branch of the library.

JUL 1 2 1982

D1500305

JUL 1 2 1982

THE WIDOWER

GEORGES SIMENON

Translated by Robert Baldick

A Helen and Kurt Wolff Book
Harcourt Brace Jovanovich, Publishers
New York and London

Copyright © 1959 by Georges Simenon

All rights reserved. No part of this publication may be reproduced or transmitted in any form or by any means, electronic or mechanical, including photocopy, recording, or any information storage and retrieval system, without permission in writing from the publisher.

Requests for permission to make copies of any part of the work should be mailed to: Permissions, Harcourt Brace Jovanovich, Publishers, 757 Third Avenue, New York, N.Y. 10017.

Library of Congress Cataloging in Publication Data

Simenon, Georges, 1903–
The widower.

Translation of: Le veuf.
"A Helen and Kurt Wolff book."
I. Title.
PQ2637.I53V4313   1982   843'.912   81-48256
ISBN 0-15-196644-3   AACR2

Printed in the United States of America

First American edition 1982

B C D E

To
Pierre-Nicolas-Chrétien Simenon

PART ONE

THE FOUR WALLS

1

He had no more of a premonition than passengers in a
train having a meal in the dining car, reading, chatting,
dozing, or watching the countryside go by a few moments
before disaster overtakes them. He walked along, without
showing any surprise at the holiday appearance that Paris
had just assumed almost overnight. Isn't it like that every
year at the same time, with the same unpleasantly hot days
when your clothes stick uncomfortably to your skin?

At six o'clock in the evening, he was still living in a sort
of innocence, which showed itself chiefly by a certain
emptiness. What could he have replied if somebody had
asked him point-blank what he was thinking about as he
ambled slowly along, head and shoulders above most of
the passers-by?

What had he seen, from Rue François-Premier, where
he had spent over an hour at the office discussing his work,
to Faubourg Saint-Honoré, where he had cashed a check,
then all the way to the *Stock Exchange Press*, and finally
from there to Porte Saint-Denis?

He would have been hard put to it to reply. There had
been some tourist buses of course, especially near the Ma-
deleine and the Opéra. He knew that because it was the
season, but not a single one had made any impression on
him, and he could not have said what color they had been.
Blue probably, and red and yellow. And on the sidewalks,
men without ties or jackets, in open-necked, short-sleeved

shirts, with Americans here and there dressed in white or cream-colored suits.

He had registered nothing specific. Or, rather, there had been one thing. On Rue du Quatre-Septembre, he had stopped for the first time, to mop his forehead, for he perspired a lot and wore the same suit winter and summer. Out of discretion, out of modesty, he had pretended to be looking at a store window, which happened to be that of a hat shop, and among the hats his eye had been caught by a boater, the only one on display, just like the one his father used to wear at Roubaix when he took his children out on Sunday mornings, holding them by the hand. For the space of a second, he had wondered, without attaching any importance to the matter, whether the fashion for boaters was coming back, whether he would follow it, and, if he did, what he would look like wearing one.

The second time, he had stopped at a traffic light and, in the stream of cars moving past at walking pace, he had followed with his eyes a man pushing a cart loaded with a packing case big enough to contain a piano. The idea of a piano had occupied his mind for a few moments; then, shaking his head at the sight, he had looked at a very scantily clad girl sitting by herself in a huge open car.

He had not linked these pictures together or drawn any conclusions from them. He had certainly seen several café terraces, and noticed the smell of beer every time as he passed. But what else could he remember, even if he tried hard? It was almost as if he had not lived.

And in his own district, where the setting was even more familiar to him, where he took his surroundings for granted, he had seen practically nothing.

To get to his rooms, on the third floor of an apartment house on Boulevard Saint-Denis, between a brasserie and a jeweler's shop specializing in clocks, he had a choice of two entrances. On the Boulevard side, a low archway, a dark, damp tunnel next to the brasserie which passers-by never noticed, led to a paved yard, six feet by nine, where, behind filthy window panes, the concierge kept a lamp burning all the year round.

He could also go along Rue Sainte-Apolline, and, just past the packer's shop, turn into a passage that looked more like the entrance to a real house.

Questioned a few months later, at the Assizes, for example, where it would be a matter of life or death, he would have hesitated to state under oath that he had gone one way rather than another.

That would not be necessary. There was no question of it. It was a matter of no consequence which way he went, or whether the concierge was in her hole or not.

The staircase was dark. The steps creaked more than most. He knew them well. He had always known the same dismal yellow walls and the two brown doors on the second floor. On the right-hand door there was an enamel plate: *Maître Gambier, Bailiff.* Behind the one on the left, you could hear laughter and snatches of songs; he knew, from having found the door open sometimes, that a dozen girls of fifteen or sixteen worked there making artificial flowers.

He went upstairs at the same slow, regular pace at which he walked. People who thought that this was his way of giving himself a certain dignity were mistaken. Nor was his gait due to his paunch or his bulk. He had set himself to walk in this way about the age of twelve, when he had grown tired of being called clubfooted by his schoolmates.

"Why don't you make a cobbler of him?" he had heard a neighbor ask his mother once. "Most clubfooted people become cobblers."

He was not really clubfooted. He had been born with one leg weaker and a little shorter than the other, and when he was still very young his parents had bought him a pair of orthopedic shoes, one of which was fitted with metal supports.

All by himself, without saying anything to anybody, he had set himself to walk in a certain way, and after a few years he had been able to wear shoes that looked like ordinary shoes. He no longer walked with a limp.

He did not think about his leg on this particular day, or about anything specific. He did not feel tired. He was not thirsty, even though he had not stopped at a café for a drink.

Neither on Rue François-Premier, at *Art and Life*, where they had accepted his designs, nor at the Blumstein brothers', where he had cashed his check, had anything unpleasant happened. Even less happened at the *Stock Exchange Press*, where, in the almost empty rooms, he had finished making up a publicity brochure.

On the landing, no instinct made him fumble for his key, which was at the end of a chain in his pocket. Jeanne would be there. He turned the handle of the door. The draft indicated that one window at least was open, and that did not surprise him either. The noise from Boulevard Saint-Denis came into the rooms, which, with their low ceilings, acted as soundboxes, but, because he was used to it, that did not worry him any more. Noise made no impression on him. Nor did drafts. And in the evening and at night, he no longer noticed the purple neon sign of the clock shop winking at regular intervals like a lighthouse.

Putting first his leather briefcase and then his hat on the drawing board, he said, out of habit:

"It's me."

No doubt it was then that everything started, for him at any rate. He ought to have heard the sound of a chair being moved in the dining room, the door of which was open, footsteps, Jeanne's voice echoing his own. He waited, motionless, surprised, but not in any way worried.

"Are you there?"

Even if she had been in the kitchen, certain sounds

6

would have told of her presence, because apart from the main room, which he called the studio, the apartment was extremely small.

He could not remember, later on, what he had thought at that moment. In the end he had gone toward the door. The appearance of the dining room had made an unpleasant impression on him.

Just as the studio, which served as his bedroom, was not a real studio, the dining room was not a real dining room either.

True, they had their meals there, but Jeanne's folding iron bed stood against the wall, clumsily camouflaged by an old red velvet tablecloth. In one corner, by the radio, there was a sewing machine, and on certain days the ironing board was brought out of its cupboard.

He ought to have found at least some sort of untidiness, according to what Jeanne had been doing that afternoon: either the cover taken off the sewing machine, revealing scraps of material and bits of thread, or else, on the table, some kind of needlework, a dress pattern of brown paper, some magazines, some peas to be shelled.

The kitchen, which was minute, with a round skylight in place of a window, was empty, and there was no saucepan on the gas stove, nothing in the sink, not even a vegetable peeler on the checked oilcloth on the table.

She had not said anything to him. She was not in the bathroom, which he had had so much trouble installing, six years before, in what had been the darkroom.

He went back into his own room—that is to say, into the studio—hung his hat up where it belonged, behind the door, over the raincoat, which had not been used for the past three weeks.

Before sitting down, he carefully mopped his forehead, his gaze wandering over the tops of the buses that, lined up end to end, formed an almost solid mass, and then falling on a human agglomeration that, at the corner of the

Boulevard, suddenly broke up to dash across the street.

To tell the truth, he did not know what to do. Sitting in his leather armchair with his legs stretched out, he stared in front of him at the clock with the copper pendulum. It said half past six. Instinctively, his hand felt on the table for the evening paper, which ought to have been there, for Jeanne usually went down about five o'clock to buy it, at the same time as anything else she needed for dinner.

It was puzzling. Not worrying yet, or alarming. It was simply a disagreeable feeling. He was not accustomed to being disappointed and he did not like his peace of mind to be at the mercy of anybody else, including Jeanne.

He lit a cigarette. He smoked ten a day. His throat was sensitive and, without being faddish, he took good care of his health. Now and then he gave a sudden start; the noises reaching the apartment did not have the same resonance as on other days. He ought to have been deep in his paper, smoking the same cigarette, the eighth, the last two being kept for after dinner.

What was missing was the sound of footsteps, movements in the kitchen, the silhouette in the doorway of Jeanne coming now and then to look silently at him.

If they said very little to one another, each knew, at any given moment, exactly where in the apartment the other was and what he or she was doing.

"She'll have gone upstairs to Mademoiselle Couvert's!" he said to himself at last, with a feeling of relief.

It was stupid of him not to have thought of that sooner. Mademoiselle Couvert, who was sixty-five and who, on account of her eyes, scarcely ever left her apartment, occupied the rooms just above theirs, and for the last four years a boy who presumably belonged to her family, an orphan, if Jeantet had understood rightly, had been living with her.

If he knew nothing more about the boy than that, it was because he listened with only half an ear to the explanations people gave him, not so much out of indifference toward others as out of discretion, out of modesty.

The boy was called Pierre, was ten years old, and often asked permission to come downstairs, where he would settle, facing Jeanne, to do his homework.

At other times, Jeanne would go upstairs to lend a hand to the old woman, who, though she could still sew, did not dare to do any more cutting out.

It was quite simple, He had only to look on the dining-room table. She was bound to have left him a note, as she usually did on such occasions: *"Have gone to see Mademoiselle Couvert. Back soon."*

He was so sure he was right that he waited until he had finished his cigarette before going to have a look in the next room. There was no note. He looked in the wardrobe. His wife did not possess so many clothes that it would be difficult to know what she was wearing that day. What was more, since she made her dresses and coats herself, he had the material before his eyes, taking shape little by little, for days and sometimes weeks at a time.

In any case, she had not dressed for a real outing, for what she called "going to town," because her two good dresses were there as well as her straw-colored summer outfit. She must be wearing the little black dress she used at home and the old shoes she used as slippers.

So she must be somewhere in the district. Or else she was upstairs and had forgotten to leave the usual note for him. He could have gone up there and knocked at Mademoiselle Couvert's door. But because he had never done that before, his action would assume too great a significance.

He could also go downstairs and question the concierge. True, she and Jeanne never spoke to one another, and going out by Rue Sainte-Apolline you did not pass the lodge. It was not the usual kind of apartment house. The concierge was not a real concierge. Most of the time, she helped her husband with his work repairing chairs in the damp little yard, and the lodge served hardly any purpose except that of receiving the tenants' mail.

He took advantage of the fact that he was on his feet to go and drink a glass of water in the kitchen, letting the water run long enough to be cold.

The idea of working or reading did not occur to him. He hesitated about sitting down again. His studio seemed less attractive than on other days. Yet heaven knows that he was familiar with every inch of it. He had installed everything in it, down to the humblest object, in such a way as to obtain the maximum satisfaction, and he had succeeded in this.

With four walls, or, rather, six, for on the Rue Sainte-Apolline side there was a recess, a sort of alcove, containing a couch that served him as a bed, he had managed to create a world that suited him well and that struck him as having been made in his own image.

The walls were stark white, as in a monk's cell, and two drawing boards, the big one and the little one, evoked the idea of a craftsman's work, slow, peaceful, harmonious.

If he did not paint Madonnas after the fashion of Fra Angelico, he put just as much fervor into designing special letters and title pages for expensive magazines like *Art and Life*, or ornamental letters and tailpieces for limited editions.

On top of all that, for several years he had been hard at work on a long and exacting task: the creation of a new type face, such as appears once every twenty or fifty years, and which would bear his name.

In printing plants and newspaper offices, people would speak then of a Jeantet, just as they said an Elzévir, an Auriol, a Naudin . . .

Certain letters, greatly enlarged, inscribed in the beautiful black of India ink, were beginning to cover the walls.

He did not look at them, any more than he looked at

the silver tops of the buses, which, seen from above, looked like whales, or Porte Sainte-Denis, which the sun was gilding like terra cotta.

He had resigned himself to sitting down again. "His" armchair, which he had finally unearthed at the Flea Market after months of searching, had quite a history. So had every object in the room, including the clock with the sea-green face and the Roman numerals of Louis-Philippe's time, which now said that it was seven o'clock.

He knew that people often took him for a spineless character, and it was true that his big body appeared to have no consistency. Though he was not fat, still less obese, he seemed to lack the rigid framework of a skeleton. All the lines of his body were curved and ill-defined, and they had already been like that when, as a schoolboy, he had got out of breath at recess quicker than the others.

People could not guess that he was just as highly strung as they were, perhaps even more so, that at the slightest emotion he felt something like physical panic. His blood no longer seemed to be following its normal route; vague, mysterious things moved about in his chest; one moment a finger became sensitive and started hurting, as if it had been seized with cramp, then all of a sudden it was a shoulder that went stiff, and the next thing was nearly always an unpleasant feeling of heat at the base of the skull.

He did not get alarmed about it, did not mention it to anybody, least of all to Jeanne. He calmed down by himself. It was a long time, in any case, since it had last happened, or else it had been very slight, brought on by some minor vexation, or more probably by some humiliation. But humiliation was not quite the right word. To be more precise, the attack came on when he had the impression that people were misjudging him, that they were treating him unfairly, that they were doing their utmost to harm him.

It would have been enough for him to say just one word.

He hunted for it and tried to summon up the courage to pronounce it, and it was the feeling of impotence that came upon him then that would suddenly bring on the attack.

This was not the case at the moment. There was nothing wrong. Jeanne would be back in a minute. He listened for the sound of her footsteps on the staircase. In his mind, he saw her coming upstairs, stopping on the landing, opening her handbag . . .

A detail suddenly struck him: he had not needed his key to get in. And he could not remember a single occasion when Jeanne had gone out without double-locking the door.

"In a district like this . . ." she used to say.

He for his part had never been afraid of burglars.

He had been waiting for her now for over an hour, which meant that she had been out even longer. Something had happened, not necessarily something serious, but something unexpected. He could not stay there any longer, in his armchair. To ease his throat, he went into the kitchen to have another glass of water; then he went out, without putting his hat on, without locking the door.

Not yet daring to go up to Mademoiselle Couvert's, he went down to the ground floor and made for the little yard where the lamp in the lodge made a yellowish patch behind the dirty window. He knocked without looking inside, since a quick glance had shown him the husband sitting with his feet in a tub beside a table already laid for dinner.

"Mélanie!" shouted the motionless figure.

And a voice coming from behind a curtain that served as a partition replied:

"What is it?"

"A tenant."

"What does he want?"

"I don't know."

This was his first surprise, and it struck him that he had made a discovery. It was true that he rarely knocked at the door of the lodge. He suddenly found two human beings living in this ill-lit hole, a few yards away from the crowds swarming along the Boulevard and the people drinking on the terrace of the brasserie where an orchestra four or five strong played on Saturday evenings and Sundays.

The woman emerged from the shadows, small, tired-looking, hard-eyed, like a suspicious animal. She did not open the door, but just pushed aside a pane of glass like a ticket-office window.

"If I had any mail for you, I'd have taken it up."

"I wanted to ask you . . ."

"Well then, speak up! What do you want?"

He already felt discouraged.

"I just wanted to know if you'd seen my wife go out. . . ."

"I don't take any notice of tenants' comings and goings, and even less of what their wives are up to."

"I don't suppose she said anything to you?"

"If she'd said anything to me, I'd have given her tit for tat."

"Thank you."

He did not say these words ironically, but out of force of habit, because it was his nature. She had just hurt him without any justification. He did not hold it against her. If anybody was in the wrong, it was he. He followed the passage as far as the luminous opening onto the Boulevard and then, to calm his impatience, went around by Porte Saint-Denis and Rue Sainte-Apolline.

It was rather like going from the front of a stage-set to the back. The same buildings looked out on both sides. On Boulevard Saint-Denis, there were attractive shop windows, restaurants with gilt decorations, and in the evening a riot of illuminated signs in all the colors of the rainbow.

On Rue Sainte-Apolline, there were tradesmen and

workers, first the packer's establishment, then a little cobbler's shop next to a laundry, where women stood ironing
all day while, on the opposite sidewalk, two or three prostitutes with very high heels walked backward and forward
in front of a hotel and some men sat playing cards in the
half-light of a little bar.

Nobody knew him. He knew every figure, every face,
from having watched them from his window, the one above
his couch.

Surely Jeanne had had time to come home while he was
walking around the building? To give himself a better
chance, he decided to take another one or two turns. In
the course of the third, he stopped outside the dairy Jeanne
patronized, which was still open. It sold not only eggs,
butter, and cheese, but also cooked vegetables for people
who hadn't the time or, if they lived in hotel bedrooms,
the right to do their own cooking.

"You haven't seen my wife, have you, Madame Dorin?"

"Not since this morning, when she came in to do some
of her shopping."

"Thank you."

"You aren't worried about her, are you?"

"No, of course not."

As he said that, he felt like crying from sheer nervous
exhaustion.

It was a case of that sort of impotence which affected
him so deeply. . . . Jeanne was somewhere around. There
was probably nothing seriously wrong: a delay, an over-
sight, a misunderstanding, a chance incident.

What was there to stop him, while he was waiting for
her, from going upstairs and eating whatever he could find
in the pantry? Or else from going into the first restaurant
he came to? Or again, if he did not feel hungry, from
reading in his armchair?

He forgot to buy the evening paper and went up to his

apartment, where there was still nobody to be found and one of the windows was taking on a red tinge. The day struck him as being longer than most. It was nearly eight o'clock and the sun had not finished setting, people on the terraces were still drinking beer and apéritifs, and men were still walking about in shirt sleeves.

Jeanne was not subject to fainting fits. It was unlikely that she had collapsed in the street, and even if she had, she was bound to have her identity card on her. For two years now, they had had a telephone in the apartment.

He stared at it on the table, frowning hard. If she had been held up, if something had happened to delay her, why didn't she call him?

Was he to conclude that, convinced that he would go and ask Mademoiselle Couvert, she had left a message for him?

He did not believe that this was the case but nonetheless he went up that part of the stairs which was unknown to him, and saw a zinc plate with the old woman's name on it and the word *Dressmaking*.

Standing on the doormat, wondering whether to knock, he heard the sound of plates and the boy Pierre asking insistently:

"Do you think I can go now?"

"I don't know yet. Perhaps."

"Do you think it's probably yes or probably no?"

"It's possible. I'd like to be able to say yes right away."

"Then why don't you?"

He knocked, feeling embarrassed at listening without meaning to.

"I'll go!" announced the child.

And, all at once, the door opened wide and the pages of an illustrated magazine on a little table fluttered in the draft, as did the hair of the old woman, who had stopped eating.

"It's Monsieur Bernard!" cried Pierre.

"Excuse me . . . I wondered whether, by any chance, my wife had left a message with you for me. . . ."

The boy looked at him with a keenness older than his years; then he looked at Mademoiselle Couvert, hesitating whether to shut the door or not.

"Hasn't she come home?" the dressmaker asked in surprise.

"No. And I can't imagine why not. . . ."

What was the use of saying anything more? Jeanne and he had certain habits that were not particularly logical and that were liable to cause a smile. Wednesday was his day, the only day he made the rounds of the firms that employed him, as he had been doing that very afternoon.

There was no reason why Jeanne, if she had some shopping to do, should not go out the same day, but in fact, to his knowledge, this had never happened once in eight years.

Besides, she rarely went outside the district, and when she did, because it was a case of more or less important purchases to be made in the big stores on Rue La Fayette or elsewhere, she talked about it for several days beforehand.

She would not have gone wearing her old black dress.

"Won't you come in for a moment?"

"No, thank you. She has probably come back while I was up here. . . ."

She had not come back, and the light in the apartment was changing with every movement of the black hands on the clock face. In the sky above the rooftops, a cold green was gradually taking the place of the pink of the setting sun, of which only a few fleecy clouds still bore some trace.

This frightened him, filling him with an almost physical dread, and, unable to stand it any longer, he took his hat from its peg, went downstairs, and plunged into the crowd, walking at a quicker pace than usual, which made him limp.

For other people it would have been easy; they would have had nothing to do but turn to their relatives, to a sister or a sister-in-law, to their friends, to their colleagues.

For them, this was out of the question. They had nobody, apart from Mademoiselle Couvert and the boy, who had watched him go with a thoughtful look.

The passers-by, in couples, in families, were taking up the whole sidewalk and advancing with the leisurely motion of a river, slowing down where the café terraces, encroaching on their path, created bottlenecks. The traffic was thinning out. Although it was still broad daylight, the lights had gone on outside the movie houses and straggling queues were beginning to form outside the box offices.

Leaving the Boulevard, he dived into quieter streets where, here and there, old people had brought chairs out on the sidewalk to enjoy the air. The street was filled with smells coming from the shops, which were still open, and voices and snatches of conversation could be heard everywhere.

He arrived at Rue Thorel, saw the gray official building, the flag hanging from its pole, the policemen's bicycles, two sergeants coming out tightening their belts. One of them looked at him as if his face reminded him of something, then straddled his bicycle without having found the answer.

He went into the police station, where, just as in the concierge's lodge, the lamps were lit, and where pipe and cigarette smoke was floating in the air. A man of uncertain age was trying to explain something across a sort of dark wood counter above which a peaked cap could be seen projecting.

"Have you got a work permit, yes or no?"

"Monsieur . . ."

That was about all he could say in French. For the rest, he was using incomprehensible words, gesticulating, and spreading out with a feverishly trembling hand papers that bore dirty finger marks and that had obviously been carried around in his pocket.

". . . told me . . ."

"Who told you?"

With a gesture of the hand, he seemed to be indicating that it was somebody very tall or very important.

"Monsieur . . ."

"Just the same, he didn't tell you that this was a work permit, did he?"

None of the papers was the right one. There were white ones, blue ones, in French and heaven knows what foreign language.

"How much money have you got?"

He did not understand the word *money*. Behind him, a young woman was stamping with impatience and making signs to the policeman.

Some bills were produced. The man understood and took out of his pocket a handful of greasy, crumpled paper money, then a few coins, which he lined up on the counter.

"That may be enough to save you from being charged with vagrancy, but it won't get you very far and you'll have to be taken back to the frontier. Where did you get that money?"

"Look here, Sergeant," interrupted the young woman, "I have to be at the theater at quarter to nine and . . ."

She was wearing an almost transparent dress.

"Go and sit over there," the policeman said to the man, pointing to a bench running along the wall.

He went, full of resignation, without understanding, wondering what they were going to do with him. He too had come from somewhere for a reason known only to himself.

Jeantet bit his lip. The woman, for her part, knew what she wanted.

"It's just to witness a signature."

"You live in the district? You've got a residence certificate?"

"Here it is, signed by the concierge."

She opened her handbag and a whiff of perfume escaped from it.

"I'm going on tour and I need a passport. So . . ."

"On tour, eh? . . . All right. Come back tomorrow morning. The Superintendent isn't here at this time of day."

Two other policemen, each sitting rigidly behind a desk, were doing nothing, were not moving a muscle.

"You, now, what do you want?"

"Could you tell me if there's been an accident this afternoon?"

"What sort of accident?"

"I don't know. . . . Perhaps a street accident?"

A man had come in, not by the public entrance but from the other side, a big fellow wearing a hat, his face shining with perspiration. He shook hands with the others, then studied Jeantet through the smoke from his pipe.

"There are street accidents happening every day. Why do you want to know?"

"My wife hasn't come home."

"Since when?"

"I left her at two o'clock."

"And what does she do?"

"Nothing . . . The housework . . ."

"For somebody else?"

"No. At home."

"Is she fifty-two?"

"She's twenty-eight."

"Then it isn't her. The one who was knocked down by

a bus on Rue d'Aboukir at ten past four is a woman of fifty-two. Posetti, she's called . . ."

Always this feeling of impotence! He could not even think of a question to ask. Nobody helped him. Every face was expressionless.

"Is she in the habit of straying?"

"No."

"Then what are you worrying about?"

As he was trying to understand, somebody spoke to him from behind. It was the newcomer, the man whose face was gleaming with perspiration and whose pipe smelled very strong.

"Say, don't you live on Boulevard Saint-Denis?"

"I live on Boulevard Saint-Denis, yes."

"On the third floor, over a clock shop?"

"Yes."

"Don't you recognize me?"

Jeantet made an effort, but for some time now everything had seemed unreal to him. He had seen that face before, that expression of vulgar self-assurance, at once good-humored and aggressive.

"Doesn't the name Inspector Gordes mean anything to you?"

He blushed scarlet.

"Yes."

"I did you a service once, although you didn't follow my advice. Well, what's the trouble now?"

"She's had an accident."

"Still the same woman?"

"Yes."

"When?"

"This afternoon."

"Where?"

"I don't know. I came here to find out."

"You mean she hasn't come home?"

He lowered his head. He could not stand it any more.

He could see smiles appearing on every face in the room, except that of the foreigner, who, sitting in the middle of the bench, was trying to discover what was wrong with his pink, blue, and white papers.

2

Perhaps they weren't really ill-natured but just saw life from a different point of view? Perhaps, indeed, it was simply a question of occupation and this at once hard and disorderly atmosphere, which Jeantet found unreal and confusing, was their everyday atmosphere?

The police, like other trades, were bound to have their own professional jargon, words that either meant nothing to other people or else had a special meaning for them alone, like face and pearl, lower case and em quadrat, to take only a few instances, at the *Stock Exchange Press.* Weren't there people to whom the press stone at a printing plant, the heavy forms, and the lead you handled with gray fingers, seemed dull, uninteresting, or sinister?

He did not blame anyone and, like the foreigner on the bench, he tried to make himself understood, to establish some sort of contact. He quickly gained the impression that he was wasting his breath and that his lips might as well have been moving noiselessly.

"Listen, Inspector . . ."

That black barrier, against which tens of thousands of ready explanations had come to grief, embarrassed him, as did the gaze of the three silent policemen, who seemed to be playing minor parts in a familiar scene.

"I'm sure she's had an accident. Perhaps it didn't happen in the Second Arrondissement. . . ."

"Have you already made inquiries in the Third?"

Their apartment house was practically on the borderline between the two administrative districts.

"No . . . I hoped that one might be able to phone from here. . . ."

The Inspector was sure to have a private office. Why didn't he ask Jeantet into it? Was it because it was a slack time of day and the others with their peaked caps needed something to keep them amused?

When he had met him, eight years before, Gordes had been a slight, almost thin man, and at first he had taken him for a reporter or a salesman. Even then he had been untidy in appearance and self-assured in manner, the sort of man you see sitting for hours in cafés, and it was probably through eating and drinking, especially drinking, that he had put on so much weight.

"Cornu, get me the Emergency Service."

In his mouth, what could have been a friendly request became an order, and he perched on the desk of the policeman in uniform, taking the receiver out of his hands.

"Emergency Service? . . . That you, Manière? . . . I thought I recognized your voice. . . . Hot, yes . . . Here too . . . How're things? . . . And the kids? . . . Mine's off on holiday with his mother at the end of the week. . . . To his grandmother's, as usual . . . Look, among the accidents this afternoon, you didn't have a woman of about thirty, did you?"

He had not taken his eyes off Jeantet and now he spoke to him.

"What was she wearing?" he asked.

"A black dress, a fairly old one."

"A black dress . . . Distinctive mark on the cheek . . . Mark, yes . . . That's right. . . ."

And speaking to Jeantet again, he asked:

"The left cheek or the right cheek?"

"The left."

"Left cheek, old man. . . . A souvenir, as you say . . .
Monsieur wasn't pleased. . . . You haven't seen anything?
. . . Everything quiet? . . . No, I've just come on. . . .
Thanks . . . Yes . . . I won't forget to tell him."

He hung up and drew on his pipe, shaking his head.

Jeantet tried again.

"Couldn't somebody have taken her straight to a hospital?"

"A report has to be drawn up in every case of an accident. You don't go into a hospital as you do into a movie."

"But what about an emergency case? . . . Suppose she's collapsed and some people who don't know her have picked her up . . . ?"

He sensed that this didn't hold water, that it wasn't what he ought to say, especially here.

"All right. Get me Hôtel-Dieu, Cornu. . . ."

Then it was the turn of Saint-Antoine Hospital and Saint-Louis Hospital.

"Are you convinced now?"

The Inspector had not done all that to help him, out of kindness, but in order to prove to him that he was right. There were other hospitals in Paris. But was it likely that Jeanne, dressed as she was, would have gone very far from her district?

He did not dare to insist. Gordes was looking at the case from a professional point of view and his thoughts found expression in the question:

"Didn't they make her pay, way back, when you picked her up?"

All these words were beside the point and conjured up nothing but a caricature of reality. Jeantet shook his head.

"But I warned you that she'd have to pay. A man doesn't let the girl who's working for him go without paying. If he did, he'd be the laughingstock of the underworld."

He had nothing to say in reply. He was in a hurry to get away. He felt certain, all of a sudden, that Jeanne had come home, and he reproached himself for having brought all this filth to the surface through his impatience.

"She didn't ask you for any money? Something in the neighborhood of a quarter or half a million francs?"

"No."

"Then she must have got hold of it somewhere else. Did she go out a lot?"

"Never."

"Have you any friends?"

He blushed a second time, and declared, without really knowing what he was saying:

"Either she's come home while I've been here, or else something has happened to her."

"Just as you like. Come and see me about it again tomorrow."

A car drew up outside the police station. A door slammed. The door of the police station flew open and two uniformed policemen pushed a couple of men into the middle of the room, one with handcuffs on his wrists, the other with his face covered with blood. Both had very dark hair and southern features, but Jeantet never knew whether they were Spaniards or Italians, for he did not stay long enough to hear them speak.

It was just a picture for him: the policemen young, immaculate in their uniforms, full of health and vitality, calling to mind athletes in a stadium, and the others, who were roughly the same age, dust-stained, their shirts torn, their eyes hard and stubborn.

The one who was bleeding did not seem to have noticed and was letting the blood trickle down from his chin onto his shirt, which was stained red with it.

Just as Jeantet was going out, one of the policemen put an open pocket knife on the counter, and the man on the bench, distracted for a moment from his papers, raised his head and gazed at the new arrivals, still looking as if he were trying hard to understand.

To understand what? Why men hurt one another?

At the door, Jeantet was surprised to find that it was still light, and he stared for quite a while at a pigeon pecking about in the gutter.

He made an effort not to walk quickly. It was best to let as much time pass as possible, for every minute gave Jeanne another chance to come home.

The streets were quieter and less crowded, the noises deadened. The proprietor of the brasserie on Boulevard Saint-Denis was surveying his terrace. He was a bald, placid little man who for a long time had been a waiter in Strasbourg or Mülhausen. Did he see the cross street, the tables, the glasses of beer, and even the sky, which was beginning to cloud over, with the same eye as his customers, who were enjoying the air?

He too would have his own language, his own way of seeing life and people. And every one of his customers, sitting there at a table in the dusk, was really living in a separate world, into which none of his neighbors could enter.

He had known that for a long time. It was because he knew it so well that he had taken care to set limits to his domain and to surround it with protective barriers. He had chosen to make it as simple as possible, so that it should be in less danger, and now, all of a sudden, from one hour to the next, almost from one minute to the next, everything had begun to collapse.

He ran up the stairs two at a time and threw open the door, as if everything depended on what he would find.

Empty!

He dropped into his armchair and, his eyes wide open, not knowing what he was staring at so intently, he remained motionless.

He was not hungry, thirsty, hot, or cold. He was not tired and he was not really unhappy either.

And yet, little by little, it became unbearable: an insidious distress, which took the form of strange twitches, mysterious movements all over his body.

"I mustn't!"

He did not realize that he had spoken aloud, in the empty apartment, into which the outside noises were still entering through the open windows. He mustn't go out searching the streets for Jeanne. His instinct urged him to do just that. He had to exert tremendous self-control to remain slumped in his armchair, more listless in appearance than he had ever been before.

If it wasn't an accident, then it was a crime. Hadn't Inspector Gordes thought of that too? Jeantet had nearly spoken to him about it. What had prevented him was the fact that the same words meant different things to the two men. Gordes's words dirtied everything.

Jeanne had not paid because he, Jeantet, had told her not to, and also because he could not have given her so much money. At that time, eight years before, he had been barely thirty-two years old; he had not yet bought the armchair, or the two drawing boards; the darkroom, which had formerly been used by a street photographer, had yet to be converted into a bathroom.

Now that he came to think of it, that had happened on a Wednesday too, for he had already picked that day to go on what he called his "rounds."

He had had dinner by himself that evening, in the half-furnished dining room, and he remembered that on his way home he had stopped at Madame Dorin's to buy some cooked vegetables.

It was summer, later in the season than now, toward the end of August, and most Parisians, especially in this district, had returned from their holidays. The windows were open, the noises much the same as today.

In those days, he used to settle down in a wicker armchair to read all the works on the great voyages of discovery that he could find at the Arsenal Library or in the bookstores. He had gone on reading late into the night, until about one o'clock in the morning, and then, with the light out, he had stayed with his elbows on the sill of the window overlooking Rue Sainte-Apolline.

There had been only two of them outside the door of the hotel, the light from which spread a rectangle on the sidewalk. The little bar, a bit farther on, had already lowered its shutters. One of the women, who was very fair-haired, was in pale blue and the other was wearing a black dress.

A man had turned the corner of the street, walking hesitantly, and had suddenly decided to cross over to have a closer look at the women. He had gone past them; the one in blue had run after him and, after a fairly lengthy discussion, had managed to bring him back to the hotel, where a light had soon gone on in one of the windows.

When, a fortnight later, the Inspector had come to talk about Jeanne, he had gone over to the window, looked meaningfully at the hotel across the street, and winked at Jeantet.

It was not difficult to see what he was thinking, but he was wrong. Rue Sainte-Apolline, the hotel, the comings and goings of the prostitutes and their customers, all this was in fact on the fringe of his world; it almost formed part of it, but in the morning he looked at the other side in just the same way, at the waiter straightening up the terrace of the brasserie and the beer barrels being rolled across the sidewalk to be sent down a chute into the cellar.

The rest had happened quickly. A man, hiding in some corner or other, must have been waiting for the street to be deserted, and Jeantet had not seen him coming. He had suddenly noticed him, a supple, silent figure, a few feet away from the woman in black, who had seen him at the same time as Jeantet and who, after seeming about to run away, had stood rooted to the spot.

The incident, which had taken place in absolute silence,

had lasted only a few seconds, and yet every movement was distinct in Jeantet's memory: the man planting himself in front of the woman, waiting for a moment, then calmly slapping her on both cheeks before she could put up her arm to stop him.

Without pausing, he had seized hold of her hair with his left hand, in a gesture that was precise rather than brutal, and, taking his right hand out of his pocket, he had struck her across the face, with surprising slowness.

Finally, with a violent shove, he had sent her rolling onto the sidewalk. Satisfied, with the air of a man who has done what he had to do, he had gone off in the direction of Rue Saint-Denis, disappearing around the corner before very long. He was just a shadow in the shadows. You could not even hear the sound of his footsteps.

Nothing moved in the street, and only one foot and one leg of the woman on the ground were lit up by the light coming from the hotel.

Who knows? If he had had a telephone at the time, perhaps all he would have done would have been to inform the police. Instead, he had put on his trousers and his jacket and, without a tie, he had gone downstairs in his slippers.

By the time he reached the opposite sidewalk, the woman was trying to get to her feet, slowly, without groaning, without whimpering. She was still on her knees, with one hand on the ground, and her eyes had traveled slowly and uncomprehendingly up the unexpected figure in front of her.

Her neck and one half of her face were covered with blood, but, like the man at the police station today, she seemed to be unaware of it.

He held out his hands to help her. Defiantly, she stood up by herself and, once she was on her feet, before thinking about her handbag, which had fallen a little farther away, she asked:

"What do you want?"

"You're hurt . . ."

"Well? What's it got to do with you?"

Just like all the rest, in fact. But this time he had not lost heart.

"You need attending to."

"I'll attend to myself, thank you."

Picking up the handbag, he had held it out to her. She had removed a handkerchief and wiped her cheeks with it, and it was only then, at the sight of so much blood, that she had felt the full impact of what had happened. Her eyes had widened and set in a fixed stare; he had just had time to seize her by the shoulders as she fainted.

His first idea had been to drag her into the corridor of the hotel, to call the night porter, anybody he could find. Just as he was beginning to do this, she came to sufficiently to protest, to struggle.

"Not here!"

"Why not?"

"They'll tell the police."

"Where do you want me to take you?"

"Nowhere."

"Do you live in this district?"

Hadn't that sentence had the same effect on the woman as certain other sentences had on him? Hadn't he just addressed her in an unfamiliar language?

She had repeated, in a tone of voice that was ironic rather than bitter:

". . . *live* . . ."

And he had said, clumsily:

"You can't go on bleeding like that. . . . There's a pharmacist's open on the Boulevard . . ."

"Yes, and a cop right opposite!"

He had looked up at his window.

"Come to my place. I'll be able to see if it's serious and if you need a doctor."

He pointed to his apartment house.

"It's over there. . . . On the second floor . . . Don't be frightened . . . !"

"Frightened of what?"

For a moment, he wondered whether she might not be drunk. She was looking at him as if he belonged to a different species of humanity from her own. And when, in his apartment, she finally saw him in the light, he thought that she was going to burst out laughing.

"Stay there . . . I'm going to get some water and some cotton. . . ."

Frowning slightly, she inspected her surroundings.

"Haven't you got a mirror?"

There was only a little one, in a metal frame, hanging from the hasp of the dressing-room window, which he used for shaving.

"Don't move . . . I won't hurt you."

He had done his military service as a medical orderly; it was easy to see that, while the wound was quite deep, the cheek had not been cut right through. In fact, there were two wounds in one, the knife blade having made a cross about two inches wide.

"All that I've got here is some iodine. . . . It'll burn you. . . . Afterward you'll have to go and see a doctor, and he'll put some stitches in."

"And report me to the police!"

"If you ask him not to say anything . . ."

"They have to. I know."

She was barely twenty years old. She was dark and dainty, neither ugly nor beautiful, and her vulgarity had something artificial about it, like her self-assurance.

"Do you know who did that to you?"

For all that he was twelve years older than she was and considered that he had reached maturity, it was she, that night, who behaved like the elder of the two.

"Forget it! Thanks just the same for looking after me."

"But you aren't going off like that?"

"What else can I do?"

"Aren't you frightened?"

Yes, she was frightened, all of a sudden, possibly because, through the window, she had just caught sight of Rue Sainte-Appolline and, on the opposite sidewalk, the blonde in the blue dress, who had taken up her position again. At the corner of the street, two men, whose cigarettes moved about in the darkness like fireflies, seemed to be watching the area.

"Is it you they're looking for?"

"I don't know."

"You don't think it would be better for you to spend the night here?"

He remembered that look of hers, more expressive of incomprehension and stupid suspicion than the clumsiest of words.

He hurriedly added:

"There's another room, behind the door. . . . I'll sleep in an armchair."

"I'm not sleepy."

"You will be soon. Your cheek doesn't hurt?"

"It's beginning to."

"I'll give you a couple of aspirin."

"I've got some in my bag."

He had pulled the wicker armchair into what had since become the dining room, and about three o'clock in the morning he had finally dropped off to sleep. It was the first time that a woman had slept in his rooms, and he found it difficult to get used to the idea, since he had always imagined that he would live alone all his life.

The next morning, she had a temperature. He had not asked her what her name was, not even her Christian name. The black dress, covered with dust, was lying on the floor beside the shoes, whose heels were twisted and whose insides were stained with sweat, while two dirty feet were poking out from under the blankets, blood had stuck her hair together in locks, and one eye was ringed with blue.

"Nobody has been here?"

"No."

"Have a look out the window. I mustn't show myself. There isn't a man strolling up and down outside, is there?"

She had lost the self-assurance of the previous night. Her nerves were on edge, and she gave a start every time she heard footsteps on the stairs.

"It's a warning."

"What is?"

"What he's done to me."

"You know him?"

A fortnight had gone by, and on the third day he had gone to a secondhand dealer's on Rue du Temple and bought a folding bed, which he put up every evening in the dining room. He had to put his legs through the bars, since it was he, at that time, who occupied this bed, which was too short for him.

She was trailing around the apartment barefooted, wearing a dressing gown of his, which she had gathered up with pins, when, one morning about eleven o'clock, there had been a knock at the door. After putting one finger to her mouth and giving Jeantet an imploring look, she had run and locked herself in the dressing room.

The visitor was Gordes, not so fat as he was now, and not sweating so much, because there was a cool drizzle falling that day. Before opening his mouth, he had made a swift inventory of the room. Pointing to the dining room, he had asked:

"Is she there?"

"Who are you talking about?"

With a scornful look on his face, he had produced his card.

"The prostitute Moussu. Jeanne Moussu. The one who was marked by her pimp a fortnight ago. What are you going to do with her?"

He had not replied, because at that moment there had been no reply he could possibly have made.

"It's Friday today, and yesterday she missed her examination for the second time running."

Jeantet asked naïvely:

"What examination?"

The other man looked at him as if he had never come across such a phenomenon.

"The medical examination. Do I have to make a drawing for you? When a woman's registered as a prostitute . . ."

Jeantet was sure that Jeanne was listening behind the door and this embarrassed him.

"What if she wanted to be taken off the register?"

"In that case, it wouldn't be any concern of mine. She'd have to apply to the Vice Squad at the Quai des Orfèvres, prove that she had a responsible guarantor and adequate means of support, and comply with a certain number of formalities . . ."

"That's possible, isn't it?"

"Oh, yes! Oh, yes! Everything's possible, as you say, even that. Have you got a regular job?"

He examined, with a mocking smile, the typographical characters with which the walls were already decorated.

"What exactly do you do?"

"I'm a commercial artist."

"Does that bring in much?"

"Enough to live on."

"You're a bachelor?"

The Inspector walked up and down, still wearing his hat, knowing just as well as Jeantet that Jeanne was behind the door. It was on purpose that he went up to it now and then, and stopped just as he was on the point of opening it.

"Just as you like," he sighed in the end.

It was then that he had leaned out the window overlooking Rue Sainte-Apolline and had glanced first at the hotel opposite and then at Jeantet's reddening face.

He had gone on right away:

"It's got nothing to do with me. . . . That trick comes off once in a thousand times, and you've as much right as anybody else to try your luck. She can go and see Superintendent Depreux, and it would help if you went with her and took your papers with you, including references from the people you work for. . . . Don't forget a certificate from the police registry. . . . And later on, when the little man turns up again, all you'll have to do is find the wherewithal to pay him."

"Pay him for what?"

"In that class, when you take a man's woman away from him, you're robbing him of his livelihood. It's only fair that you should pay him compensation."

The door had opened and Jeanne had said:

"Drop it, Bernard. The Inspector's right."

They had been using the familiar *tu* form of address with each other for only three days, and the first time it had happened he had spent hours afterward walking the streets trying to clarify his thoughts.

In the next eight years, he had passed the Inspector several times in the street, and every time that he could he had avoided his gaze.

For months, Jeanne and he had lived, so to speak, shut up as if in a fortress, and when she had finally gone out with him, she had all but fainted.

Only eighteen months later they were married, at the town hall of the Second Arrondissement, the witnesses being two strangers whom Jeantet, on the advice of a municipal employee, had gone to find in a nearby bistro. They acted as witnesses for births as well as for marriages and deaths, and the mayor or his deputy pretended not to recognize them.

The neon sign went on blinking, buses still went by

from time to time, cars drove faster along the practically empty streets, and the magnified voices of the passers-by rose in the silence of the night.

There were sure to be some women opposite, two or three, new ones or old ones, at the door of the hotel, where now and then a window lit up.

He did not doze off, did not close his eyes, but went on following, as on a diagram of an anatomical plate, the twitchings of his nerves, the movements of his blood in his arteries.

It wasn't true! His whole being protested at the idea! It was inconceivable that after eight years Inspector Gordes should be proved right and he, Jeantet, wrong. It was not a matter of a dispute between two men. It was not a question of conflicting opinions. The problem went beyond them, went beyond Jeanne too, and in Jeantet's eyes took on a cosmic significance. The world was called in question once more, and life too, not just that of a man and a woman, but life itself.

For eight years, they had nourished with their substance the space comprised within these walls, they had made of this anonymous dwelling a distinctive world, of which every element, every molecule, bore their mark and which was truly theirs.

Not his. Not hers. Theirs.

The rhythm of their days was not governed by clocks or by the rising or setting of the sun. It was the most intimate essence of their lives, their own rhythm in fact, which had created a routine that obeyed no rules, submitted to no influences.

Thus, at this very moment, he ought to be reading, listening at the same time to Jeanne getting ready for bed, and she would come and kiss him, almost as shy as in their first month together, and murmur:

"Don't stay up too late."

Hadn't the Inspector seemed to be insinuating just now,

that this would never happen again, because of her, because she didn't want it to happen again?

Old Mademoiselle Couvert was asleep overhead, in the same room as Pierre, who could be heard moving about barefooted the nights he walked in his sleep. Other tenants, even farther up, whom he scarcely knew by sight, were doubtless also asleep. The bailiff's office was empty, because he lived in an apartment in the suburbs.

It was unfair. It was false. He had just found the word and he was sure that he was right: there was a false ring about the whole business. It was inadmissible that Gordes, despite appearances, should be right after all.

Jeanne had not gone. She had not cut herself off from him voluntarily, deliberately. It was true that they had never paid anybody off, but, contrary to what the Inspector thought, nobody had ever come and asked them for it.

They had lived for a long time on the *qui vive*, constantly expecting to hear a knock at the door. But the man whose name Jeantet had not wanted to know had never shown up.

If he had been prevented from coming, for example by a prison sentence, and he had just been released, wouldn't the police have told him?

False! He had to find out what was false at the bottom of it all. Jeanne was not in a bedroom somewhere with some man, or by herself. She was not wandering the streets. She had not taken a train either, in the little black dress she wore every day and her old shoes.

Gordes had called the three nearest hospitals. There were others in Paris, and Jeantet got to his feet, heavy, clumsy, like a man who has been drinking, put the light on, and, blinking in the glare, started turning the pages of the telephone directory.

"Hello . . . Beaujon Hospital? . . . Excuse me, Mademoiselle . . . I should like to ask you . . ."

"Is it an emergency?"

"No . . . Could you tell me if you admitted a young woman named Jeanne Jeantet this afternoon?"

"For an operation?"

"I don't know."

"How do you spell the name?"

"J for Joseph . . . E for Emile . . ."

Then Bichat Hospital, Boucicaut Hospital . . . All this paralyzed his mind. He patiently repeated: "No, Mademoiselle . . . I don't know. . . . J for Joseph . . . E for Emile . . ."

Every time, he apologized, said thank you.

"Hello . . . Bretonneau Hospital? . . . No, Mademoiselle, it isn't an emergency. . . . I just wanted to know . . ."

He stared fixedly at the dining-room door, and his eyes grew misty.

"Thank you, Mademoiselle."

He forgot to smoke the last two cigarettes of the day.

"Hello . . . Broca Hospital? . . ."

Then Broussais . . . Chauchard . . . Claude-Bernard . . . Cochin . . . Croix-Rouge . . . Dubois . . . Enfants-Assistés . . .

A gust of wind made the door in front of him tremble, and he would not have been surprised to see a ghost come in.

Laënnec . . . La Pitié . . . Lariboisière . . .

Hundreds, thousands of beds, with people who were sick, injured, dying, bodies that were being opened and corpses that were being taken downstairs in elevators . . .

His sister, Blanche, did not work in a real hospital but at La Maternité on Boulevard du Port-Royal. She was a midwife. She was three years older than he was. She lived by herself in a Montsouris Park apartment, and since his marriage to Jeanne they had seen nothing of one another.

He had a brother too, an elder brother, with a wife and three children who lived in a little house at Alfortville. A stronger, stockier fellow, he was a locomotive engineer for French National Railways.

He even had a mother, at Roubaix, who, by marrying again, had fulfilled her life's ambition, for her second husband ran a bistro by the canal.

These people had nothing in common with him, or with the apartment on Boulevard Saint-Denis, in which none of them had ever set foot.

Saint-Joseph . . . Saint-Louis . . . No! The Inspector had already telephoned Saint-Louis Hospital. . . . Salpêtrière . . . Tenon . . . Trousseau . . .

The last of them all: Vaugirard.

"J for Joseph . . . E for Emile . . ."

This time, when he opened his mouth to say thank you, it was a sob that came out, and he let his head fall on his folded arms.

3

About three o'clock in the morning, there must have been a big fire in the neighborhood of Rue des Petites-Ecuries or Rue du Paradis, as far as he could make out. He had not gone to bed. He was still in his armchair when he heard two fire engines passing underneath his windows, then another one, more powerful than the first two, a quarter of an hour later. When, later still, the big ladder truck had gone past, with its helmeted men lined up in pairs, he had gone to the window and had seen a final vehicle taking a party of officials to the scene of the fire.

The boulevards were practically deserted and, at the foot of Porte Saint-Denis, a stray cat meowed every time it heard footsteps in the distance. In the direction in which the firemen had disappeared, there was no smoke or fire to be seen above the rooftops, but now and then he made out a distant murmur and a sort of rumbling noise which he could not quite identify.

In the course of the night, he counted five police cars which went through the district with their sirens wailing. None of them stopped in the immediate vicinity. The nearest incident must have occurred in Place de la République, for he heard the sound of a shot coming from that direction.

If he did happen to drop off, he was not conscious of doing so; his eyes were wide open when the sky turned pale and the first trash men started dragging garbage cans along the sidewalks.

A powerful sedative, or a narcotic of some sort, Novocaine, for example, or even opium—he could not tell, because he had never tried one—would doubtless have put him in the same state. It was not, strictly speaking, insensibility. His body, to the contrary, was more sensitive than ever, especially his eyelids. He was nonetheless numb, mentally and physically, and there were long periods during which everything became confused, both his thoughts and his feelings.

In this way he had got through the night. There was another day. Then another night. In the end, time disappeared, the hours faded away, there was nothing and there was everything, a void peopled with expectation and figures, which were now gray, now colored.

What time was it when he went and made his first cup of coffee in the little kitchen where he had forgotten where everything was kept, it was so many years since he had stopped living alone? There was already sunshine, scattered noises, everyday life beginning outside, and when, standing up, he dropped three lumps of sugar into his cup, stirred with the spoon, and brought his lips near the scalding liquid, a word leaped to his mind, a word he could not remember using before, the word *widower*.

He suddenly felt absolutely certain that he had become a widower, and this struck him as a mysterious condition.

He heard footsteps overhead and recognized them as those of Pierre, who was so fond of coming to do his homework facing Jeanne.

And now he realized that he did not possess a single picture of his wife, not even a passport photograph. They had never needed a passport. They never did any traveling. The idea of taking his wife on holiday had not occurred to him again since one summer, the year they were married, they had gone to Dieppe and had had tremendous difficulty finding a bed, in a crowded hotel, where they had not been given so much as a look of sympathy.

He could not swim. Not once in his whole life had he put on a bathing suit. Animals, cows, bees, and dogs frightened him, and in the country, however much he reasoned with himself, he was always tormented by the feeling that he was surrounded by hostile forces.

He waited until eight o'clock before calling the police station. Inspector Gordes, who, that particular week, was on night duty, had already gone.

"I'll put you through to Inspector Maillard . . ."

He had a sympathetic voice.

"My colleague has put me in the picture. . . . No news, of course . . . Give me your phone number and I'll call you if I hear anything at all. . . ."

The result was that he stopped listening for footsteps on the stairs and fixed his attention instead on the black instrument on the table, which might start vibrating at any moment.

There were footsteps all the same, coming from upstairs about half past nine, youthful, skipping footsteps, followed by a timid knocking. He went to open the door to the boy, and took the opportunity to pick up the bottle of milk and the loaf of new bread that were outside on the landing.

"I'm not disturbing you, am I?" asked Pierre, trying to look as if he were simply paying a call, but without being able to refrain from glancing inquisitively all around him.

He did not dare to ask the question. Jeantet nonetheless declared:

"She hasn't come home."

"Do you think she's had an accident?"

He did not say that he had called every hospital in Paris.

"I don't suppose it's anything serious, do you? If it was serious wouldn't they have come and told you?"

Embarrassed by the idea of leaving right away, the child stayed for a few minutes, doing nothing and saying nothing, like somebody visiting a sick person, and when he had gone, rushing down the stairs in relief. Jeantet went and lay down fully dressed on the couch, where he finally fell asleep. When he woke up, the noises on the terrace down below told him that it was lunchtime; he had a drink of milk and ate some bread and butter with a slice of cold veal he found in the meat safe, which hung outside, above the yard.

He refused to go out, to push his way through the crowds in the streets, looking for Jeanne. He washed and shaved, tried to do some work in the course of the afternoon, and failed. It was all so utterly senseless. Only in his armchair did he feel at ease, with his legs stretched out and his eyes half shut.

The telephone still did not ring, and he was as isolated as if, as the result of an epidemic or a mass exodus, he had been the sole remaining inhabitant of Paris.

How many hours did this go on? On Wednesday, it had been just after six in the evening when, returning from Rue François-Premier, the Faubourg Saint-Honoré, and the *Stock Exchange Press*, he had found the apartment empty. That evening he had still felt optimistic, because he had taken a few turns around the block of buildings, imagining each time that Jeanne would be home when he got back.

Wednesday night . . . Then a whole day spent doing nothing, remaining in suspense . . . Not even thinking, for he really did not think about anything, and, paradoxically, when pictures came to his mind, they were chiefly pictures of his childhood, at Roubaix, near the canal, where his mother queened it now behind the bar of a café . . . He knew the café well, because it was already there when, at the age of three or four, he had begun playing marbles on the sidewalk. . . . He could remember distinctly the smell of gin mingling with another smell, that of the pitch with which they coated the barges. The bargemen who came out of the café and trod on the marbles used to smell of pitch and gin.

Six in the evening again, and, down below, the terrace packed with customers sweating and drinking beer.

He made himself some more coffee; the words *coffee* and *widower* were linked in his mind like pitch and gin in his memory. Wouldn't he have to go through all these movements again every day now, and get accustomed once more to the kitchen, where he had to hunt around to lay his hand on the sugar or the matches?

There were three eggs left in the larder, and when night fell he finally summoned up the courage to break them into the frying pan.

Inspector Gordes, who had come back on duty, still did not telephone. This evening, outside the hotel on Rue Sainte-Apolline, there was a girl in a white outfit whom he had never seen before and whose figure and brown hair reminded him slightly of Jeanne.

When the crowds came out of the movie houses late in the evening and made their way toward the Métro, he decided to call the police station.

"The Inspector's making his rounds. We still haven't heard anything."

Could it be that Gordes, in order to prove that he was right, had begun looking for Jeanne, not dead, but alive?

He refused to undress, but slept just the same, fully clothed, on the couch. Like that, he did not deliberately take refuge in sleep, which he would have considered cowardly. Besides, he could still hear the buses, see the neon light going on and off, make out the voices of passers-by and the whistles of trains in the Gare de l'Est, which meant that the wind had changed.

At six in the morning, thirty-six hours had elapsed. It was Friday. He had to count the days to make sure. Pierre came again about eight o'clock and sat down on a chair, looking more solemn than the day before.

"Aren't you doing anything to find her?"

"There's nothing I can do."

"What about the police?"

"I told the police yesterday. . . . No, the day before yesterday . . ."

He kept getting the days mixed up. In front of the child, he walked back and forth, pretending to be busy, with a disagreeable feeling that the boy's eyes were looking at him reproachfully. He even went so far as to say, just as if he were answering an accusation:

"I've done everything in my power to make her happy. . . ."

Why did Pierre say nothing?

"Don't you think she was happy?"

The yes was not categorical enough for his liking.

"Have you ever seen her cry?"

He suddenly realized that Jeanne had had longer conversations with the boy than with him. Often, working in his studio with the door half open, he had heard them chatting quietly, and now he wondered what they could have had to say to one another.

"Have you ever seen her cry?" he repeated suspiciously.

"Not very often."

"She cried now and then?"

"Now and then . . ."

"Why?"

"When she didn't do things properly . . ."

"What things?"

"I don't know. . . . Her work . . . Anything . . . She'd have liked everything to be perfect. . . ."

"What did she say to you about me?"

"That you were kind."

There was no warmth in his voice, and it annoyed Jeantet to see the child looking at him like a judge.

"She didn't think the life we led was monotonous?"

"She thought you were kind."

"And what about you?"

"I think so too."

"She didn't know anybody in the district whom I've never seen?"

He instantly regretted his words: he was in the process of committing a kind of treason, of putting himself, without wanting to, on Gordes's side. He hurriedly answered his own question:

"No . . . If she had known anybody, she would have told me everything. . . ."

He would have liked Pierre to confirm that this was so, but the boy broke off the conversation.

"I've got some shopping to do."

For it was he who did the shopping for the old dressmaker, and, on school days, he could be seen running from one shop to another with his list and his string bag, before school began.

At a certain point in the morning, Jeantet noticed that the clock had stopped, and wound it up again. He was leaning out the window to see the right time by the big clock hanging over the shop below when he heard a bell ringing, and, with his head outside, he did not realize right away that it was the telephone at long last.

It was seventeen minutes past eleven. He had been waiting for forty-one hours.

"Bernard Jeantet?"

"Yes."

"This is the police station of . . ."

"I know."

He had recognized Inspector Maillard's voice, his way of talking. He waited, not daring to ask the question, and there was a fairly long silence.

"Well, I think this is it. . . . I've called Gordes at his home, and he's going over there right away. . . . He thinks it would be best for you to go there as well, to identify her. . . ."

"Dead?"

"Yes . . . That is . . . Well, you'll see. . . ."

"Where is she?"

"Rue de Berry, off the Champs-Elysées . . . You'll see a hotel on the right with a queer name. . . . The Hôtel Gardénia . . . You'd better hurry, because from what I've been told, they won't keep her there for long. . . ."

Well, that was that. Jeanne was dead. He could see no rhyme or reason in it. It was senseless. He went out, taking his hat and forgetting to shut the door, which the draft slammed to while he was going downstairs. He passed the concierge's lodge, and saw the lighted lamp at the end of its cord, the man repairing a chair out in the yard and smoking an old pipe that had been mended with a bit of wire.

He got into a red taxi with a low ceiling and bumped his head.

"Rue de Berry."

"What number?"

"Hôtel . . ."

How stupid of him! He had forgotten what it was called!

"The name of a flower. . . ."

"I know. . . . The Gardénia."

He might as well have been crossing a foreign city, because he did not know which way the driver was taking him. The streets were blocks of sunshine in which he saw, as if through a magnifying glass, light-colored clothes and laughing faces.

The taxi stopped. He noticed a uniformed policeman outside a glass door with a canopy over it. There were no curious onlookers, no newspapermen or photographers either; just two little black police cars at the curb.

A rather small but light lobby, with marble-lined walls, a mahogany reception desk, and evergreens in the corners, and on the stairs a handsome red carpet held in position with brass rods.

Inspector Gordes was standing by the desk and, when Jeantet arrived, was talking to a silver-haired lady dressed in black silk.

"Come this way, Jeantet. . . . To save time, I asked my colleague to call . . . I was at home when they told me."

"It's she, is it?"

"I think so."

He had his hat on and his pipe in his mouth, but the expression on his face was different, the look in his eyes too, which gazed at Jeantet as if there were something he could not quite understand.

The black gate of the elevator closed behind them; they were carried smoothly up to the fourth floor, where, on the landing and in the corridor, three or four men and two chambermaids in striped dresses stood eying one another silently.

"Room 44," murmured the Inspector, so that he would know where to go.

If the hotel was not particularly big, its atmosphere struck him as cozy and refined. On the white doors, the numbers had been cut out in brass or bronze, and here too there were evergreens and a red carpet.

"The local superintendent has been here for quite a while. . . ."

Gordes paused for a moment.

"I'd sent the description out to every arrondissement, asking them to let me know if anything turned up. . . . Unfortunately, they didn't tell me right away. . . . The police doctor has already gone. . . ."

He seemed to be making sure that his companion was strong enough to stand up to the shock that lay in store for him. Before opening the door, he himself mopped his forehead and took off his hat.

"Keep a tight hold on yourself. . . . It isn't very pretty. . . ."

They had been obliged to throw the windows wide open,

on account of the smell. To prevent the people opposite from looking in, they had closed the shutters, which admitted only a few thin rays of sunlight. The ceiling light was on. A powerful disinfectant had been sprayed all through the room.

Jeantet saw the first picture in a big mirror, so that for a moment the sight was unreal, rather like a photograph that has been superimposed on another. When at last he turned around, slowly, to look at the big low bed, he stood rooted to the spot, speechless, motionless.

He saw a white dress he did not know, feet wearing expensive new shoes, and hands of an indefinable color, with dark-blue nails, holding a bunch of withered roses. Other flowers were scattered over the bed, as if a procession had passed by, and the petals that had fallen off formed a kind of paste here and there.

He wanted to say:

"It isn't she. . . ."

Or, rather, not say it but shout it, then rush out of the room waving his arms for joy. Unfortunately, the Superintendent removed the towel covering the face, and Jeantet stood there, dumbfounded, staring at Jeanne. It was she, her eyes open, her hair spread out on both sides of the pillow, a bloated Jeanne, whose mouth and chin were covered with a thick brown liquid.

"Come along . . ."

He was taken by the arm. He was pulled out of the room. On the landing, he noticed a stretcher and a coarse sack. The elevator went down. Evergreens brushed against him. They were out in the street, out in the sunshine, he and Gordes, and the Inspector, who was still holding him by the elbow, pushed him into the half-light of a little bar.

"A couple of brandies!"

Jeantet tossed down his glass.

"Another one?"

He shook his head.

"Another for me."

Gordes drank it, paid, and took his companion outside to where a black car was standing.

"They've put it at my disposal till midday. . . . We might as well take advantage of it. . . . We'll be more comfortable in my office. . . ."

On the way to the police station, he refrained from asking any questions, and kept on smoking, crossing and uncrossing his thick legs.

They did not go through the room with the long counter where they had met last time. The Inspector took him up a dusty staircase and across an office where some men were working in shirt sleeves. He pushed open a door.

"Sit down. I warned you that it wasn't very pretty. She hadn't thought that the flowers would speed up decomposition. They never think of things like that. Just the same, you recognized her, did you?"

Jeantet had not taken a single step in the direction of the bed, but had allowed himself to be led away without giving himself time for a silent farewell, he had been so relieved to get away from the sight of that bloated face on the pillow.

"How do you feel?"

"I don't know."

"You don't want me to have a drink sent up?"

"No, thank you."

He still remembered to say thank you, and made a mental note of the fact.

"Did you bear me a grudge the other night?"

"Why?"

"On account of what I said to you."

"She's dead."

"Do you know how she died?"

He shook his head.

"She swallowed the contents of a tube of some narcotic or other. They found the tube in the bathroom and, in a glass on the bedside table, a few drops of a very strong dose."

He heard himself asking:

"*When?*"

"We'll know after the post-mortem."

The word made no impression on him, produced no reaction.

"In any case, there's no doubt it's suicide."

"Why?"

"Because she was alone in the room."

"Since when?"

"Wednesday."

"At what time?"

"She arrived at three o'clock."

Jeantet continued insistently:

"Alone?"

"Alone. At five o'clock, she ordered a bottle of champagne."

He did not understand any more. The office, for all its administrative solidity, lost all reality. A stage-set in a fog. Patches, lines, noises. He repeated:

"Champagne?"

It was grotesque. They had never drunk champagne together, not even on their wedding day. The idea had never occurred to him.

"If you had looked in the left-hand corner of the room, you'd have seen the bottle standing, nearly empty, with a single glass on a little table. The men of the Eighth Arrondissement have been working on the case since nine o'clock this morning."

At five o'clock on Wednesday, he had still been at the *Stock Exchange Press*, bending over the press, and that was the time when Jeanne should have gone downstairs to buy his evening paper as well as anything she needed for dinner.

"The dress?" he said, looking up and frowning.

"Which one? If you mean the black one . . ."

"She was wearing her black dress . . ."

"She gave that, and her old shoes too, to the chamber-maid."

"When?"

"I don't know. I'll ask my colleagues. They're sure to ask you to go to the police station over in the Eighth Arrondissement."

"And the white dress?"

"That was hers. So were the others."

"What others?"

"The other dresses. They found four in the wardrobe, as well as underwear, dressing gowns, shoes and stockings, and two or three handbags."

He felt like standing up, losing his temper, and shouting at the fat man, despite the fact that he was talking to him quietly and without the slightest suggestion of irony:

"It's a lie!"

It was all falser than ever. Already Jeanne's absence had failed to fit in with reality as he knew it. As for her death, it was becoming increasingly incongruous.

"Look, Jeantet, your wife had been living in that room for a long time. Over a year."

"Living in it?"

"She had been occupying it, if you like. She kept her things there; she went there regularly."

"Was it in her name?"

He nearly corrected what he had said to:

"Was it in *my* name?"

"In a man's name."

"Whose?"

"For the time being, I'm not allowed to tell you."

"He was her lover?"

"According to the hotel staff, they met there once a week. . . ."

"But she's never slept anywhere except at home!"

"You don't have to spend the night at the Gardénia. It's a place we know very well, where a good many couples meet in the afternoon."

"In that case, that man may have . . ."

"No. I can guess what you are going to say. The staff have been questioned. He didn't set foot in the hotel on Wednesday, or yesterday, still less today. . . . They called his home. . . . He isn't in Paris at the moment. . . . Indeed, he's a long way from France. . . .

"Nobody went into Room 44 except the delivery boy who brought the flowers, which your wife ordered herself, and, at five o'clock, the waiter who served the champagne. . . . She insisted that she wasn't to be disturbed. . . . Just the same, the next day—that's to say yesterday, Thursday—toward the end of the morning, the chambermaid knocked at the door and, getting no reply, concluded that she must be still asleep. In the afternoon, another maid took over. Since nobody had given her any instructions, she didn't bother about Room 44, thinking it was empty. . . . It was only this morning that the first chambermaid got worried. . . ."

"So she's probably been dead since Wednesday evening?"

"We'll know about that tonight, or tomorrow morning at the latest."

The Inspector knocked his pipe out onto the floor.

"That's all I can tell you. Perhaps you may learn some more from my colleagues of the Eighth Arrondissement. Perhaps you, yourself, if you look through her belongings and her papers . . ."

"What papers?"

"Her correspondence . . . Her address book . . ."

"She never wrote to anybody."

"That doesn't mean that nobody wrote to her."

"She never had any mail."

In their apartment, where every object had its special

place, how could she possibly have hidden anything at all from him? They lived together from morning till night, from night till morning; the doors between the various rooms were left open all the time, and each of them, hearing the slightest movement made by the other, was aware of his or her every gesture.

He remembered, for example, that once, about five o'clock, Jeanne had said to him from the next room:

"Careful, Bernard. That's your ninth cigarette."

She could not see him. She simply heard the matches being struck and smelled the smoke.

He stood up, his face expressionless.

"You don't need me any more?"

"Not for the moment. As I said back at the hotel, keep a tight hold on yourself."

Gordes added, as he was taking him through the office next door:

"Remember . . . one case in a thousand . . . if that!"

It wasn't true! Jeantet said nothing, because he knew that it was useless, that nobody would believe him. Yet he had his own ideas on the subject and he was sure that it was the others who were wrong.

Perhaps Jeanne really had taken the sleeping medicine. It was quite likely, seeing that she was dead. Perhaps too she had drunk a bottle of champagne, all by herself, to give herself courage. And it was also possible that it had been her idea to scatter roses on the bedspread and to take a bunch of flowers in her hand before . . .

He stopped short on the stairs. *She was dead.* He was only just beginning to realize the fact. Even that morning, in the bedroom on Rue de Berry, it had been too far removed from reality.

Coming out of the door, in front of which there was a row of bicycles, he nearly knocked over a little man going in, and turned around to see that it was, as he had thought, the foreigner with the papers in every conceivable color.

He was returning to the attack, alone against the world, against the laws and the regulations, against the whole bureaucratic machine, stubbornly confident of the rightness, the truth, the logic of his course.

Curiously enough, he did not think about the lover. Of everything that had been revealed to him, that had made the least impression on him. What worried him most of all was the dress, the black dress and the old shoes, which Jeanne had given to the chambermaid. He would have liked to get them back, and if he had dared, he would have hurried over to the hotel to claim them, to buy them back if necessary.

She had been dressed in white. She had died in a dress he had never seen on her, and she had arranged her hair in a style that was unfamiliar to him.

She could have left the black dress in the wardrobe, or in a corner, with the shoes. Would that have made any difference to her?

Another idea struck him in the queue. It was lunchtime. He had to go back to Rue de Berry right away, to claim the letter. For he was certain that Jeanne had not gone without writing to him. Everything was going to become clear.

They had not thought of giving him the message. Perhaps the hotel people had not realized who he was. He stayed out on the bus platform, feeling almost reassured, now that he was on the point of knowing the truth, and, when he got out of the bus, he found himself walking with his old long, rather deliberate steps.

There was no policeman outside the door any more. He went in. In the place of the silver-haired woman who had been there in the morning, there was a much younger man with brilliantined hair, who was checking the account book as if he were the proprietor.

"Can I help you?"

"I am Bernard Jeantet."

The name seemed to make no impression on him.

"Yes?"

"I came here with the police this morning to identify the body. . . ."

"Did you leave something behind?"

"The person who died was my wife."

"I see. Forgive me."

"I am practically certain that she left a letter for me, a note, a message. . . ."

"You'll have to ask at the police station about that, because it was the police who made an inventory of the contents of the room. They took away a certain number of things and put seals on the door."

"You weren't there at the time?"

"I wasn't even in the hotel."

"You don't know who was there when the police arrived?"

"The chambermaid for that floor, certainly, since it was she who . . ."

"Is she still here?"

"I'll call her."

Without taking his eyes off Jeantet, the man spoke into the house telephone.

"She's coming right down," he said.

It was one of the women Jeantet had seen that morning, in uniform, on the landing.

"Monsieur Jeantet would like to ask you a question."

"I recognize Monsieur."

"Do you know if the police found a letter in the bedroom?"

"A letter?" she repeated, assuming a thoughtful expression.

"Or a note . . . A piece of paper . . . You were the first person to go in there, weren't you?"

"Yes . . . I actually . . . But I'd rather not talk about it, because I haven't really got over it yet. . . . A letter,

you say? . . . I was in such a state. . . . Still . . . Now
you mention it, I think I do remember something. . . .
Have you asked the gentlemen from the police?"

"Not yet."

"I would if I were you. . . . It's the champagne bucket.
. . . I've an idea there was something in front of it, on
the tray, something square and white, like an envelope.
. . . Wait a minute! . . . I can remember one of the inspectors picking it up, glancing at it, and slipping it into
his pocket. . . ."

"You don't remember which one?"

"Oh, at one time there were eight of them in the
room. . . ."

"Thank you."

Jeantet went toward the door, then came back and
slipped a tip into the maid's hand.

"Oh, you shouldn't. . . ."

All that he had to do now was to claim his letter. He
had been right after all. She had written to him, and
everything was going to become clear.

4

He would have been greatly surprised if, two hours earlier, for instance, when he was coming out of the nightmare of Room 44, or else the day before when, in his apartment, he was waiting, motionless, for Fate to decide what to do with him, and silently begging it to act quickly—he would have been surprised and indignant if he had been told that he would be lunching that day on the terrace of a smart restaurant, which turned out to be quite expensive, on Rue de Ponthieu.

He had not intended to do so. He had gone first of all to the police station of the Le Roule district, a stone's throw from the Hôtel Gardénia on Rue de Berry. There he had found the same atmosphere as in the police station in his own district, the only difference being that he counted eight people, five very young boys, all dressed in much the same way, and three girls, sitting on the bench.

For a moment, he had been afraid that they would ask him to sit down in the place that was still free at the end of the bench. He had hesitated about going up to the counter, for fear of giving the impression of somebody claiming an unfair advantage.

"My name is Bernard Jeantet. I am the husband of . . ."

". . . the suicide case, I know. You've already received your summons, have you?"

It was starting all over again.

"What summons?"

"I thought I saw a summons being made out in your

name just now. A messenger took it with the others. Unless I'm mistaken, the Superintendent wants to see you tomorrow morning."

"I haven't come to see the Superintendent. I just want to have a word with the inspectors who are dealing with the case."

"They've gone to lunch. Unless Sauvegrain . . . Wait a moment."

He shouted in the direction of a half-open door through which the noise of a typewriter was coming:

"Is Sauvegrain still there?"

"He went off five minutes ago with Massombre."

"Is it on a personal matter, Monsieur Jeantet?"

"Yes, I think so. . . . I want to find out something about what happened in that room. . . ."

The Sergeant frowned and muttered:

"Oh, yes . . ."

Then, as if this were no concern of his, he added:

"Come back at two o'clock then. . . . Or preferably a bit later, because they've had a busy morning . . ."

It was when he got out in the street again that he felt hungry all of a sudden, something that had not happened to him for three days. He caught himself looking longingly at the restaurants he passed, and on Rue de Ponthieu he succumbed to the temptation offered by a terrace with tables covered by red cloths. The fact that there were only three people, three men, lunching on the terrace reassured him.

There was nothing to eat at home. His appointment at the police station, at two o'clock, did not leave him enough time to go back to Porte Saint-Denis and do his shopping. What is more, he had not yet organized, or even thought of organizing, his life as a widower.

It was an idle period, an interval, a meal that did not count. He experienced a curious feeling sitting down all by himself, then examining the duplicated menu the waiter handed him. The prices gave him a shock but, once again, this was an exception, outside the normal routine, both the one that had been in operation before and the one that was about to be instituted. There was no danger of this establishing a precedent.

It was a long time, several months in fact, since he had last had a meal in a restaurant, because he felt a repugnance, perhaps even a sort of fear, at the idea of going outside their way of life, such as it had become established, outside the limits that had gradually taken on the face of frontiers.

Feeling awkward, not to say ridiculous, he ordered the hors d'oeuvre.

"With melon and Parma ham?"

He did not dare say no, any more than he dared to refuse the kidneys that were recommended to him.

The three men at the next table were talking about a trip two of them were going to make that afternoon. They were leaving for Cannes, and it was something to do with an American car that had to be exchanged at a certain point on the route. Was it a stolen car? Turning toward the inside of the restaurant, he thought he could see something suspicious about the other customers too, and all through the meal one of the women sitting on the stools at the bar kept looking at him as if she were waiting for some signal.

It made a considerable impression on him to find himself once more in a world he had almost forgotten, or, rather, that he had never really known except through the newspapers.

How many people did he know in Paris, out of the millions of human beings among whom he had lived for so many years? He had known his brother Lucien and his sister Blanche, when they were children; he had seen them later on, Lucien a married man and the father of a family, in his house at Alfortville of which he was so proud, and

Blanche a midwife who had never married and who surrounded herself with an atmosphere of mystery.

For the past eight years he had seen nothing of them,
although he had not quarreled with them. One might almost say that he had forgotten to go and see them.

On Rue François-Premier, at the *Art and Life* offices, he
met journalists, critics, and artists every Wednesday, and
sometimes well-known authors, who sat as he did in the
waiting room. Most of them were on more or less friendly
terms with each other and chattered away while he stayed
quietly in his corner, with his briefcase or his big portfolio
beside his chair.

He waited until it was his turn to be received by M.
Radel-Prévost, the assistant editor, a handsome, smartly
dressed man, in an impressive office with silver-framed
photographs of his wife, his son, and his daughter everywhere. Together with the magazine, his family was his
chief interest in life, and at the end of the day he sped
away in a sports car to join them twenty miles from Paris.

Some of the photographs had been taken by a swim-
ming pool, probably the one at his house.

They shook hands and discussed the appearance of an
article or the balance of a double page in color, but they
never touched on personal matters. Only once, M. Radel-
Prévost had asked him:

"Have you any children?"

"No."

"Ah!"

Jeantet had quickly added:

"I should like to have had some."

Perhaps it was true. He was not sure. Jeanne, if she had
wanted children, had not dared mention it to him, knowing that he could not give her any.

Here, a few yards from the Champs-Elysées, his own
district seemed so far away that he felt quite lost. He could

have sworn that the passers-by, both men and women, were dressed differently, spoke another language, did not belong to the same race as the people on Boulevard Saint-Denis. Now and then he looked at his watch for fear of being late, just as if he had a real appointment.

He knew Mademoiselle Couvert too, of course, and was aware that she was the oldest tenant in the apartment building, that she had been living there for forty-one years. But he did not know what her relationship was with the boy, or the latter's surname.

On Faubourg Saint-Honoré, where they handled the advertising for a certain number of luxury stores, he never saw, except accidentally through a half-open door, the bosses, the Blumstein brothers. Everybody spoke of them familiarly as Monsieur Max and Monsieur Henry. He himself was content to go to the end of a corridor, a long way from the conference rooms and offices where clients were received, to see a bald little man who had been a journalist for many years and who wrote the copy and the headlines that Jeantet had to design. He was named Charles Nicollet and had become Monsieur Charles.

After leaving him, every week, Jeantet went and knocked at a little window in another corridor, and the cashier asked him for a couple of signatures before giving him a check for the work he had delivered the previous week.

Could he claim to know Monsieur Charles? The latter took indigestion pills, and he had tufts of red hair in his ears and nose. Where and how he lived, with whom, why, and in the hope of what, Jeantet had not the faintest idea.

As for the *Stock Exchange Press*, a sort of anonymity reigned there; men in long gray work coats, with skin as gray as the lead they handled all day, showed him a certain friendliness, but a strictly professional friendliness.

It was his turn to stop being Monsieur Jeantet, in order to become, for them, Monsieur Bernard. They respected him, and no doubt envied him too for not being shut up all day under the blue-green glass roof and for having the right, after an hour or two's work, to go out into the streets.

He knew nobody else, nobody at all. Silhouettes. Faces. The woman at the dairy shop, Madame Dorin, and her husband with the brown mustache, who went off to the Central Market at five o'clock every morning, their red-faced maid, who delivered the milk, the butcher, the bad-tempered woman at the baker's, the Alsatian proprietor of the brasserie, a whole crowd of people, of course, but with no more consistency than if they were in the photographs of children lined up in rows that are taken at the end of every school year.

He knew Jeanne. And now there was somebody who didn't know her and who, out of professional habit, classed human beings in separate categories, claiming to know her better than he did.

She was dead, wasn't she? And hadn't Inspector Gordes been sure, on Wednesday evening, that she was alive? Well then?

This morning, he had been rather more human, because you always talk in a certain way to people who have just suffered a misfortune. Yet at the last moment he had been unable to resist making a final allusion to his famous *one case in a thousand.*

Jeantet ate his lunch. He watched the passers-by. He went on listening, without appearing to do so, to the conversation of the three men at the next table, who had ordered Armagnac with their coffee. He himself, who normally drank very little wine, emptied the moisture-covered carafe of white wine without noticing.

He still refused to think about the problems that were going to face him on his return, later in the day, to the apartment at Porte Saint-Denis, when he took possession, so to speak, of his solitude. He had to settle the question of the letter first.

He arrived at the police station at five past two. The

Sergeant who had seen him before glanced up at the clock. "You're a bit early. . . ."

On the bench he saw the same people, the same faces, in the same order; one of the young men was asleep, with his head resting against the wall, his mouth open, and the neck of his shirt gaping wide.

"Come this way . . . I'll take you to their office."

He went through a wicket and was shown into a big room furnished with half a dozen tables. There was nobody there. The Sergeant pointed to a chair.

"Sit down. They won't be long."

On one of the tables, where a typewriter had been pushed to one side, he was surprised to see dresses, underwear, and shoes piled higgledy-piggledy, as if in readiness for a move or a journey. He did not dare get up to go and have a closer look. The door had been left open, and he preferred not to look as though he were prying. Were they the clothes Gordes had mentioned to him, the ones that had been found in the wardrobe?

They were as different from those Jeanne usually wore as the restaurant where he had just lunched was from the drivers' restaurant on Rue Sainte-Apolline. They were all silky, flimsy, bright, and floral; they reminded him more of magazine photographs of actresses on the stage than of women you passed in the street.

The shoes had such high sharp heels that it must have been impossible to walk in them; one pair was silver lamé, with some slippers beside them in old-rose velvet trimmed with white swan's-down.

He mopped his forehead, wondered whether to light a cigarette, and finally decided not to, although there were ashtrays full of butts on all the tables.

He heard voices in the next room.

"There's somebody waiting for you in the office . . ."

"Who is it?"

There was some whispering. They were talking about

64

him, the husband, the widower. Two men came in together, whom he was practically certain he had seen in the morning, and he got to his feet.

"Inspector Massombre," said one of them, sitting down at his desk, while the other went toward a closet at the end of the room to hang his jacket inside.

"The Superintendent wants to see you tomorrow morning at nine. The summons must have reached your home by now, because it was sent by motorcycle."

The Inspector put a cigarette in his mouth and held out his pack.

"Do you smoke?"

"Yes. Thank you."

For his part, Jeantet held out a lighted match. The Inspector was younger than Gordes and smarter, a smartness that reminded him of his neighbors in the restaurant.

"It seems there's something you want to ask me."

"Were you at the hotel this morning?"

"Sauvegrain and I were the first to arrive."

Judging by the glance he gave, Sauvegrain was the one who had just taken off his jacket and was beginning to type with two fingers.

"In that case, it's probably you who have got the letter?"

Jeantet did not have his back completely turned to Inspector Sauvegrain. He could not see him clearly either. He was just a silhouette to him, right on the edge of his field of vision. Yet he had a definite impression, almost a conviction, that Sauvegrain was feeling his pockets. Besides, the noise of the typewriter stopped for a moment.

Massombre looked surprised.

"What letter are you talking about?"

"The one that was on the little table, next to the champagne bucket."

"Have you heard anything about that?"

"Heard anything about what?"

Surely it was in order to gain time that the other man repeated Massombre's words?

"A letter that was found next to the champagne bucket."

"Found by whom?"

"Found by whom?" repeated Massombre, speaking to Jeantet once more.

"I don't know. I'm sure that my wife wrote me a letter."

"Perhaps she mailed it?"

"No. It was seen on the little table."

"Who saw it?"

"The chambermaid."

"Which one?"

"I don't know her name. Dark, rather stout, middle-aged, with a foreign accent."

"And it was she who told you about the letter? You mean you've been back to the Hôtel Gardénia?"

"At twelve o'clock . . . A few minutes after twelve . . . And then I came straight here and the Sergeant told me . . ."

"Have you got the inventory, Sauvegrain?"

"I'm just typing it out now. Do you want the rough draft?"

Sheets of paper covered with writing in pencil. The Inspector's lips moved as he looked through the list. You could guess the words. So many dresses. So many night-dresses. So many pairs of shoes. So many panties and brassieres. Three handbags . . .

"I can't see any mention of a letter. . . ."

At that very moment, Jeantet turned his head and caught Inspector Sauvegrain feeling in the pockets of his jacket in the closet. Was it just a coincidence? Wasn't he trying to put him off the scent when he took out a handkerchief?

"I'm sorry, Monsieur Jeantet. I just can't see what that chambermaid was talking about. Have you got the statements there, Sauvegrain? A woman with a foreign accent:

that must be the Italian maid, Massoletti, if I remember rightly. . . ."

He was given some more sheets of paper, and his lips started moving again.

"She didn't tell us anything about a letter. What exactly did she say to you? Wait a minute! You asked to see her, I suppose? And you were the first to mention a letter?"

"I was sure that my wife . . ."

"In that case she probably said she'd seen one so as not to upset you."

"She saw an inspector slip an envelope into his pocket."

"Does she know which inspector? Did she describe him to you?"

"No."

"She stated quite definitely that it was an envelope she saw?"

Beads of sweat broke out on Jeantet's forehead, for with every answer he felt that he was losing ground.

"Not exactly, but . . ."

"Listen. We have no reason whatever, seeing that you are the husband, for keeping anything from you. Are you married under the joint estate system? That's one of the questions the Superintendent will ask you tomorrow morning."

"We haven't got a marriage contract."

"Then it's a joint estate. In that case, everything you see over there, on that table, belongs to you."

He pointed to the heap of dresses and underwear.

"As soon as all the formalities have been completed, you can . . ."

Jeantet shook his head.

"It's just the letter I'm interested in."

"We'll keep on looking. We'll do everything we can to find it. . . . Sauvegrain! Will you make sure a letter hasn't got mixed up with the pile of clothes."

Another inspector came in.

"You've arrived just at the right moment, Varnier. . . . Did you see a letter this morning at the Gardénia?"

"What letter?"

"One of the chambermaids says there was a letter on a piece of furniture."

"On the little table, next to the bottle of champagne," said Jeantet, feeling that they were trying to make his letter more improbable and insubstantial.

"Can't say I noticed it."

Sauvegrain, who had been running his fingers through the silky fabrics, announced:

"Not the smallest scrap of paper here."

"And in the handbags?"

"Not a thing. In fact, I can't even see an identity card."

"But my wife had one."

"In one of these handbags?"

"No. In her own bag."

"And where is her bag?"

"I don't know."

"She didn't leave it at home when she went off?"

"No."

"Was there much money in it?"

"A few hundred francs."

"You'd better make a note of that, Sauvegrain."

"I have."

"And put it into the report."

Massombre wore the expression of a man expecting trouble and was looking at Jeantet in a way that was at once polite and disgruntled.

"Rest assured that we'll put our hands on that letter, if it exists."

"It exists, all right."

"While you're here, you might tell us if your wife has any relatives."

"Her parents, and some brothers and sisters."

"In Paris?"

"At Esnandes, near La Rochelle."

"You're taking this down, Sauvegrain?"

"Yes. How do you spell it?"

He spelled it out.

"What's their name?"

"Moussu . . . The father's a mussel farmer."

"What's that?"

"He breeds mussels on stakes on the seashore."

"Do you know him?"

"I've never met him, or his wife either."

"Where were you married?"

"At the town hall of the Second Arrondissement."

"The parents didn't come to the wedding?"

"No."

"They were opposed to the marriage?"

"They'd sent their consent in writing."

"Their daughter never went to see them?"

"Not in the last eight years. I don't know about before."

"She hadn't any relatives in Paris?"

"She's spoken to me about a brother who's a dentist in the suburbs."

"She didn't go to see him either?"

"Not to my knowledge."

"There's nobody else?"

"Four or five sisters and another brother, all in Charente-Maritime."

"The parents will have to be told before the funeral. Will you see to that?"

He had not given the matter a thought. The word *funeral* made him frown, for it suggested alarming complications to him.

"How is it all arranged?" he asked.

"What do you mean?"

"Tomorrow . . . after the . . ."

"After the what?"

"Inspector Gordes said something to me about a post-mortem."

"Yes, that's tonight. Tomorrow morning, as soon as you've seen the Superintendent and signed a few papers, you can take the body away."

He felt embarrassed at being under the scrutiny of the three men, who all appeared to consider him a weird phenomenon and now and then exchanged conspiratorial glances.

He was tempted to ask:

"What am I supposed to do with it?"

He said nothing. The question was nonetheless written in his eyes. His hands were moist. He felt as helpless as he had on the day when, stark naked and ashamed of his big body with its excessively white skin, he had appeared in front of the army doctors for his medical examination, to the accompaniment of derisive laughter.

"Were you born in Paris?"

"No. Roubaix."

"In that case you haven't got a plot in a Parisian cemetery?"

He shook his head in dismay.

"Then it all depends on you and the family. On you first of all, because, as the husband, you've got all the rights. If you take on the responsibility, you could have her buried in the Ivry cemetery, and in that case I'd advise you to see an undertaker as soon as possible so that he can deal with all the formalities. If the family prefer to take her back to Charente and you agree, then you'll have to see about the transport arrangements, and at this time of year, what with the heat and the holidays, that won't be an easy matter. Indeed, considering the state of . . . of the . . ."

He did not dare say "corpse."

". . . considering the circumstances, I rather doubt whether the railways will agree."

By now, Jeantet was looking at them through a curtain of perspiration which had formed on his eyelashes.

"As for the starting point of the funeral, that's for you to decide, whether the actual burial takes place in the provinces or at Ivry. Do you intend to take her back home?"

Unprepared as he was, he found it difficult to understand what Massombre was saying. He was still thinking of the past, of their life in the apartment at Porte Saint-Denis, of the letter, and they had asked him specific questions to which he could find no answer.

"I'm not asking you to make your mind up right away, and in any case it's no business of mine. If I took the liberty of mentioning it to you, it was just so that you could think about it. Generally speaking, relatives don't like a funeral to start from the morgue. . . ."

Massombre stood up and held out his hand. The other two remained seated. Just as he was going out, he looked straight at Sauvegrain and felt sure that the latter deliberately bent his head over his typewriter.

At lunchtime, he had felt perfectly all right, almost in touch with the outside world, and it had seemed to him that the transition would not be too difficult. Since he was going to be a widower from now on, he would try to adapt himself to his new condition, without losing Jeanne for all that, but keeping her place for her. That was something he had not tried to explain to them, feeling sure that they would not have understood.

And now he had been struck down yet again. Fortunately, to save him from going under completely, he had various things to do, the first being to go into a post office and write out a telegram in spiky letters:

MONSIEUR AND MADAME GERMAIN MOUSSU

AT ESNANDES CHARENTE-MARITIME

JEANNE DEAD STOP AWAIT INSTRUCTIONS FOR FUNERAL STOP

BERNARD JEANTET

He could think of nothing else to say to them, no formula to add. He did not know them. He went down Faubourg Saint-Honoré, just as he had done on Wednesday, but this time without stopping at the building in which the Blumstein brothers' offices occupied two floors.

He had promised to let them have on the following Wednesday a piece of work that was urgently needed and that he would have to do, not the next day, obviously, because of his appointment with the Superintendent and whatever happened as a result, but probably on Sunday.

He remembered an undertaker's he had seen on the Boulevards, and he spent over half an hour there, coming out with his pockets full of brochures and lists of current prices.

He had not allowed them to wrest any decision from him, except for an order for an oak coffin, and the employee he had seen had promised to go in person to the morgue, a place with which he seemed to be familiar, to measure the body.

They said "the body." They talked about "the deceased." It struck him as peculiar, but the words did not shock him, did not arouse any kind of feeling in him. They might just as well have been talking about a total stranger.

Earlier in the afternoon, at the police station on Rue de Berry, when they had appeared to be offering him a choice between two cemeteries, he had very nearly shouted impatiently at them:

"Do what you like with her!"

As for the employee at the undertaker's, he must be convinced that Jeantet was a hard-hearted man, probably delighted to be rid of his wife.

Here and there, people regarded him as different from other human beings, an eccentric, a phenomenon, and because he had not had the courage to hold out to the bitter end, it was practically certain that, the next day, they would bring the body to his apartment.

The idea shocked him, but he would have been unable to say why.

Contrary to what they might imagine, it had nothing to do with the business of the hotel and the suicide.

Possibly if Jeanne had died in his arms, at home on Boulevard Saint-Denis . . .

No! Not even then . . . The man at the undertaker's had shown him photographs of mortuary chapels and black hangings with silver initials to put over the door of the apartment house. But which door? The dark hole, next to the brasserie, on the Boulevard side? Or the Rue Sainte-Apolline entrance, facing the hotel?

The man had also mentioned a table of a certain size for the coffin, hastily adding that if Jeantet did not have one, they would provide trestles.

In which room were they going to put all that? In the studio? Or in the dining room, which seemed more logical, seeing that it was Jeanne's domain? But wasn't the dining room too small?

And what was it all for? For him? He would be all alone, for he did not know how long, circling around a coffin flanked by two lighted candles. . . .

He felt hardly any inclination to go home yet. He had not forgotten the letter. He kept thinking about it more than ever now that he had certain suspicions, if not any actual evidence.

It was true that he had questioned the Italian chambermaid for some time before she had remembered the letter, or a piece of paper, or an envelope; she didn't know exactly what. But hadn't she recalled, of her own accord, the gesture of an inspector picking the thing up from where it was lying next to the champagne bottle, glancing at it as if to read what was written on it, and slipping it into his pocket?

Jeantet was not suggesting that there was anything remotely suspicious about this. He was making no accusations. The gesture was no doubt quite natural and mechanical. There had been several of them searching the room, looking for clues, and putting to one side anything that might come in useful for their report. They had taken away the dresses, the underwear, the shoes, and the handbags. They had sent the glass and the empty tube to the laboratory. They would see about the letter later on. . . .

The proof that he was not mistaken, that it was not simply his imagination, was that Sauvegrain had been embarrassed, at the police station, when the letter was mentioned. He had made his colleague repeat his question, when he must have been listening attentively to what was being said. He had put his hand to his pocket, and, a little later, Jeantet had caught him looking in the closet, where he had pretended to have gone for a handkerchief.

The truth of the matter was that he had taken the letter and could not remember where he had put it. He refused to admit it. He would no doubt go on looking for it everywhere, but if he failed to find it, he could be depended on to deny energetically that he had ever laid eyes on it.

Jeantet was determined to bring him to bay. He would take steps, if necessary, to confront him with the chambermaid, and there was every likelihood that the latter would recognize him.

They could keep the body if they liked, but he wanted his letter. It belonged to him. He did not possess a single photograph of Jeanne. He would never recover the black dress, or her old handbag, which had disappeared with her identity card.

He was ready to accept all that, provided that he had the letter.

He kept on walking, without realizing that passers-by were turning around to look at him because he was ambling along, with his long, easy stride, without seeing anybody, looking straight ahead, so far into the distance and so fixedly that some people were drawn out of curiosity to follow the direction of his gaze, and were disappointed to discover, instead of some extraordinary sight, nothing but rows of houses, a patch of stormy sky, buses, cars, and thousands of human beings, tall or short, fat or thin, dressed in dark or light clothes, and scurrying about in all directions.

This all disappeared at once, as if through a trap door, when he crossed the gloomy yard where the concierge's husband was still busy mending his chair and started climbing the staircase of which his feet knew every step.

The summons that had been slipped under his door was yellow. He picked it up, hung his hat on its peg above his raincoat, sat down in his leather armchair, and, stretching out his legs, looked at the wall.

5

That night, he was able to sleep in his bed, undressed and between sheets, since there was nothing left for him to wait for. It was on account of Mademoiselle Couvert that he had not dined at home, as he had intended to, because he would have to get used to preparing his meals and eating by himself again. Just as he had been about to go downstairs to buy provisions in the local shops, Pierre had knocked at the door. Still sitting in his armchair, he was mentally recapitulating the list of things he needed, and deciding what he would say to Madame Dorin, the baker, and the butcher, if they asked him any questions.

"Come in, Pierre."

The boy did not move, but stayed in the doorway, his hand on the door handle, looking at him as if he had become a different man, a strange creature, and in an impersonal voice he said:

"Mademoiselle Couvert asks if you would please come to see her."

He had run back up the stairs. Jeantet had followed him more slowly and, finding the door shut, had thought it best to knock.

"Come in."

The old woman's voice was not the same as usual either. He felt that something unpleasant was going to happen. He gathered that she had been crying, for she was still sniveling and was holding a handkerchief in one hand. In front of her, her steel-rimmed spectacles, with their thick lenses, were lying on an open newspaper.

He had never liked the smell of this apartment, or the dressmaker herself, for that matter, but because of Jeanne, and Pierre too, he tried not to show it.

She did not look at him, keeping her head turned toward the paper, on purpose, for she was the kind of person who never does anything without meaning to.

"When did you hear about it?" she asked.

"This morning."

"And you didn't come up to tell me?"

She wiped her nose and her eyes.

"I had to wait till Pierrot read the paper to me before I knew!"

Standing in the window recess, the boy was still gazing at Jeantet, with a curiosity that was hostile.

"I was sitting here all the time, worrying myself sick. I kept sending the child to find out if there was any news. And then, all of a sudden . . ."

"I'm sorry. I've had a lot of things to do. I've been out practically all day. . ."

"Did they tell you if she suffered?"

He felt ashamed at not having thought of asking, did not know what to say, and continued defending himself clumsily.

"You know, there were so many formalities to go through. . . ."

"What does she look like?"

He shot a glance at Pierre and did not answer. Did she take his silence for indifference?

"When are they bringing her home?"

"Nothing has been decided. I have to see the police Superintendent tomorrow morning. I've sent a telegram to her parents."

"Have you told her brother?"

"I don't know where he lives."

"At Issy-les-Moulineaux."

"Was it she who told you?"

"She often talked to me about him, and also about a married sister living in England."

"She's got a married sister in England?"

"Yes, and a good match she made too. Her husband's a big landed proprietor who rides to hounds."

He knew nothing of all this, and, instead of feeling sorry for him on that account, she seemed to hold his ignorance against him. Perhaps there was no truth in these stories about her brother and sister. With him too, in the beginning, she had started by telling stories. . . .

"She didn't talk so much to me as she did to you," he murmured, thinking that this would please her.

He was mistaken. The old woman's face hardened, as if she knew a lot more but preferred to keep quiet.

"I did what I could to make her happy. . . ."

He gave the impression of defending himself. It was a mistake. Pierre's sharp eyes darted from one to the other, as if he understood everything. Mademoiselle Couvert was silent for a moment, then found the retort she was looking for.

"She didn't even try to be happy. . . ."

Perhaps he made another mistake in not asking her exactly what she meant. She had not spoken at random. She was obviously expecting him to ask her some questions, and heaven knows what she had in store for him in the way of answers.

As he remained standing there without saying anything, she sighed:

"Ah, well!"

Then, pointing to the paper, she asked:

"Have you read what it says?"

He had read nothing. He had not had the curiosity to

open a paper for the past three days. He glanced at the brief paragraph devoted to the event, at the bottom of page three:

Jeanne Jeantet, née Moussu, a married woman of 28 with no children, living on Boulevard Saint-Denis in Paris, has committed suicide in a room in a Rue de Berry hotel by swallowing the contents of a tube of sleeping pills.

There was no mention of the champagne or the dresses. But the paper added:

Before lying down on her deathbed, the unfortunate woman covered it with roses, and she was found holding a big bunch in one hand.

He did not stay any longer with the old woman. She made no effort to keep him. She had said what she had to say, and he realized that from now on relations between them would be increasingly chilly.

If this failed to disturb him, he nonetheless regarded it as a portent. He was being cold-shouldered, for no particular reason, as if he were being held responsible for what had happened.

He had not had the courage to face the woman at the dairy, let alone the grim-faced baker's wife, with her steel-blue eyes set in a face of impressive whiteness. All the shopkeepers would have read the paper or heard the news.

The police too had looked at him in a peculiar, ambiguous way. Was it because he had not found the proper attitude to adopt on such an occasion?

He chose to dine instead in a little restaurant near Place de la République, where the main course was written on a slate and the waitress had dirty legs and a black dress that hung on a tired body. He ate a sort of spinach stew, followed by some sour plums. It was all the same to him. He went on staring straight ahead, and this was not because he was thinking. To tell the truth, he did not feel that he was anywhere in particular. He was not in the real world, but somewhere between the past and the future. In other words, there was as yet no present.

He turned back the bedclothes, undressed, and drew the curtains, hearing the prostitutes' heels tapping along the sidewalk opposite, always taking the same number of steps in each direction.

The problem of the funeral worried him and was beginning to assume alarming proportions. Yet he finally fell asleep and, when his alarm clock went off, at seven o'clock, he could remember nothing of the night.

There was some ground coffee left in the box, not much, just enough for two cups. He found the bread and the milk on the landing. Since there was no more butter in the larder, he took some of the apricot jam that Jeanne used to buy for herself, because usually he never touched it.

The sky had turned an almost uniform gray. If storms had blown up elsewhere, there had been none over Paris, and the air was hotter and more stagnant than ever. Flies were buzzing around with an unpleasant noise and sticking to the skin.

On his way across the yard, he bent down at the window to ask the concierge, who was sorting the mail:

"There isn't a telegram, is there?"

"If there had been, I'd have brought it up to you."

As he was walking away, she came out of her hole. She too had read the paper.

"When are they bringing her home?"

"I don't know."

"I thought a funeral had to take place within three days."

She did not offer him her sympathy. Nobody had thought of offering him sympathy. He was a widower but not a real widower. Was it possible that people, without knowing him except by sight, were capable of sensing this?

The Superintendent of the Le Roule district received him politely but with marked coldness. He had obviously been warned that Jeantet was quite likely to stir up trouble over his wretched letter, real or imaginary.

He had before him the police doctor's report confirming that it was a case of poisoning by the consumption of a massive dose of barbiturate and giving the time of death as between seven o'clock and nine o'clock on Wednesday evening.

About eight o'clock in fact—that is to say, when Jeantet was talking about his wife to Inspector Gordes at the local police station.

For him it had just been beginning then, whereas for her it was all over.

The Municipal Laboratory confirmed that the glass found on the bedside table had contained a powerful dose, and the Records Office, which had examined it afterward, had found nothing on it but the dead woman's fingerprints.

"As you can see, Monsieur Jeantet, there can be no doubt at all that it was suicide. Have you brought along your marriage certificate, as I asked you to in the summons?"

He had a look at it.

"According to the hotel staff, the things found in the bedroom belonged to your wife and therefore pass automatically to you. They will be handed over to you in exchange for a receipt as soon as you like. All that remains for you to do is to notify your town hall of your wife's death, and it will help if you give this form to the clerk."

At last Jeantet was able to ask his question.

"Have they found the letter?"

"I've been told about this letter you keep asking for, and I've questioned the inspectors myself. I was on the spot yesterday morning. I was one of the first to arrive, together with my secretary. I've every reason to believe that nothing had been disturbed at that point, and I saw no sign of any letter."

"The chambermaid . . ."

The other man, expecting this objection, interrupted him.

"I know. The Massoletti woman was questioned yesterday afternoon."

The Superintendent paused and looked at him.

"What did she say?"

Jeantet felt that the whole of this conversation had been carefully prepared.

"That you had given her a handsome tip and that she wanted to please you."

"I tipped her afterward."

"That isn't the impression one gets from her statement. In any case, she declares that she doesn't know anything and that she didn't see any of my men pocketing a letter in Room 44."

"I'm not accusing anybody. I just think that . . ."

"We'll drop that for the moment, if you don't mind. I've got some other people to see and not much time at my disposal."

It was at that point that he signed his name, he didn't know how many times.

"Are you taking her personal effects?"

"No."

"When are you coming to collect them?"

"I don't feel like collecting them."

They had put him out of countenance. He was more determined than ever not to throw in his hand. First of all, he had to finish with what they called "the body."

He had hoped to have had a telegram the previous evening from Jeanne's parents in reply to the one he had sent them, and their silence worried him. Admittedly the man at the undertaker's had told him that it was all for him to decide, the mortuary chapel, the funeral arrangements, the Ivry cemetery, unless he left everything to the parents, if they expressed a desire to take charge. . . .

Before going to the town hall of the Second Arrondissement, he made a detour by way of Boulevard Saint-Denis.

"Still no telegram for me?"

The husband had presumably gone to deliver his chair, for there was no sign of him in the yard. The lamp was lit, as usual. The concierge was peeling potatoes.

"No. Two people, a man and a woman, have been here asking for you."

"Did they give their name?"

"They just said they were your wife's parents."

"Where are they?"

"They stayed for quite a while on the landing, and then in the yard, whispering to each other. Finally they went off, after asking me why the body wasn't here. I didn't know what to answer. They didn't look any too pleased."

"Are they coming back?"

"They didn't say."

He walked to the town hall, on Rue de la Banque, went into the big building, and followed a series of arrows, coming at last to the registry office and finally to a door marked: *Registration of Deaths*.

An old couple, a man and a woman, each as short and stocky as the other, was waiting silently outside this door as if they were mounting guard. He felt them examining him from head to foot as he went past, pushed the door open, and went along a sort of corridor to a window set in a frosted-glass partition.

The couple followed him and, when he gave his name to the clerk, the woman said:

"I told you it was him!"

The clerk seemed to know what it was all about.

"This lady and gentleman have been waiting for you for some time," he explained. "It seems there are some questions you've got to settle with them before carrying out the usual formalities."

The woman stated bluntly:

"We are Jeanne's parents."

And to her husband, poking him with her elbow, she said:

"Go on, talk to him, Germain!"

His face was burned brown by the sun and the sea. You could tell that he felt uncomfortable in his black suit, his starched shirt, and his highly polished shoes, which were obviously pinching his feet.

"We read the paper when we arrived at the station this morning," he began. "We took the night train because we couldn't start any earlier and with the other train you have to change at Poitiers. . . ."

She interrupted him, with an almost threatening expression.

"The long and the short of it is that we found out that our daughter had committed suicide, something that has never happened before in our family. You'll never get anybody to believe that she was happy, going off like that to a hotel to do herself in. I always wondered why she didn't write and why she never came to see us. Anyhow, nobody will be able to say we've left her in this filthy city, where she's never been happy. . . ."

She rattled off this speech all in one breath, then shot a satisfied glance at her husband and added, calling the clerk to witness:

"I've already told this gentleman that, even if we have to appeal to the highest authorities, they're going to give her back to us, so that she can be decently buried in her own village, where at least there'll be somebody to put flowers on her grave. . . ."

Jeantet said simply:

"All right."

He had a lump in his throat. The clerk looked surprised.

"You agree?"

He shrugged his shoulders.

84

"It's still necessary for you to register the death."

"I've brought the papers."

Like the foreigner at the police station on Wednesday, with the difference that here his own papers were found to be in order. Apparently there was even one too many, and the clerk, at once intrigued and afraid of making a mistake, called the Eighth Arrondissement police station to ask for an explanation.

While he was filling in the blanks on the various forms, Jeantet murmured for the Moussus' benefit:

"By the way, I've ordered the coffin."

"That was the least you could do, wasn't it?"

"Where do you want it delivered?"

"Well, where is she now? Is she still at the . . . What do they call it, Germain?"

"I've forgotten."

"Yes, she's still there."

"Then I suppose they'll do everything there."

"And afterward?"

"What do you mean, afterward? You'll send the body to us at Esnandes and that's all there is to it. Isn't that what was agreed?"

A little earlier, when she had been talking about transporting the body, she had added:

"Never mind what it costs."

Finding, contrary to all expectation, that he was putting up no resistance whatever, she took advantage of the fact to put the cost of transport on his account.

"All right."

He was in no mood to argue, feeling relieved at not having the coffin in the apartment and at avoiding a funeral which would have attracted the whole district.

"And her things? What's going to happen to them?"

"What things?"

"Her clothes, her dresses, everything she's got. It would all come in useful for her sisters."

She was disappointed in her husband, who had not had the courage to say all that they had agreed between them.

"Didn't you want to ask a question, Germain?"

"Oh, yes . . . About the money . . ."

"What money?"

"She must have had a bit of money. . . . And some furniture . . . Like anybody else."

"She came to me with nothing but the dress she was standing up in."

"But at that time she'd already been working for two years. . . ."

What was the use of saying anything? The clerk called him and asked for his signature.

"Will you sign as witness?" he asked the father.

"You think I ought to?"

"If this gentleman tells you to . . ."

She trusted the clerk, but not Jeantet, this son-in-law of hers whom she had never seen before and who had driven their daughter to suicide.

The couple did not take leave of him in the lobby. Outside on the steps, they still seemed to be sticking to him, and Jeantet wondered why.

"Well, what about the dresses?"

"Come along with me."

All three of them walked along together. Madame Moussu looked at the shops with a critical eye; climbing the stairs to the apartment on Boulevard Saint-Denis, she shook her head pityingly.

The apartment did not impress her, but she spotted the sewing machine the moment she went in.

"I suppose that belongs to Jeanne? As it happens, one of her sisters, who has just got married at Nieul, needs one. . . ."

It was decided that she would take the machine, together with the dresses, which she had inspected unenthusiastically.

86

"Is that all she had to wear?"

And to her husband she said:

"A fat lot of good it does, coming to live in Paris!"

Jeantet hesitated about taking them to the police station in Rue de Berry to give them the clothes that had been found in the hotel bedroom. The sisters would no doubt have found them more to their liking.

"How are we going to manage all this, Germain?"

"I suppose I'd better go and look for a taxi?"

"You'll find one right outside on the Boulevard."

As soon as he had gone out, his wife launched an attack on another front.

"I hope you aren't thinking of coming to Esnandes for the funeral!"

"I hadn't thought about it yet."

"The people at home wouldn't appreciate seeing you crying over the coffin of a woman you made so unhappy that she had to go and kill herself. . . ."

For the first time since six o'clock on Wednesday evening, he smiled, a mirthless smile, but one that roused the good woman to indignation for all that.

"Is that all you can find to say to a mother?"

The husband came back up the stairs, quite out of breath.

"Come along, Germain. The sooner I'm out of here, the better I'll like it. I feel as if I'm suffocating. You take the machine. I'll carry the rest."

He watched them go off, loaded with booty, and the woman turned around to shoot a final, menacing glance at him.

"Above all, hurry up about sending the body. By express service! . . ."

On the floor below, there was a bailiff on one side, and on the other the girls who made artificial flowers, probably for funeral wreaths. This had never occurred to him before. The half-blind old woman above him bore him a grudge because Jeanne, to use her own words, *didn't even try to be happy*.

At the time, he had registered the words, and that was all. Now he wondered exactly what Mademoiselle Couvert had meant. He had no time to think about it just now. It would be best to finish with the formalities first, and keep his promise to the people at Esnandes who were his in-laws.

The man at the undertaker's was disappointed at losing the order for the mortuary chapel and a funeral in Paris. He made no secret of his disapproval.

"If that's really what the family want . . ."

He only half-believed it, and suspected his client of getting rid of an irksome task.

While Jeantet looked through a magazine in the waiting room, he telephoned first to French National Railways, then to his colleague at La Rochelle, and finally to the morgue.

"The railway people raised a few objections but agreed in the end. You're lucky. The coffin will cost rather more, because it has to conform to certain requirements. It will leave at five o'clock this afternoon by express service, and tomorrow morning it will be at La Rochelle, where a hearse will be waiting to take it to Esnandes. Have you got the exact address?"

"No. I imagine that Germain Moussu, mussel farmer, at Esnandes, will be enough."

"I shall have to ask you to pay in advance. If you'll just wait a moment . . ."

He did a few sums, consulted his price lists, telephoned to some other organizations, and then had to call French National Railways again and add taxes and tips.

Finally he handed Jeantet a long bill.

"Will you pay by check?"

"No."

He had the money on him and counted out the notes, which the employee counted all over again.

"Are you taking the five o'clock train too?"

He shook his head and went off without caring what impression he left behind.

This time, he could feel certain that it was all over, that he had got rid of the *body* and could resume his private conversation with Jeanne. Yet it was he who put off this moment he longed for.

He had just set in motion, on payment of a larger sum of money than he had expected, machinery that, without any need for further intervention on his part, would return to the cemetery at Esnandes the girl who had set off for Paris ten years before.

All the necessary signatures had been given and every tip provided for, including the one for the village choirboy. Henceforth he, Bernard Jeantet, had no part to play in this business, and in any case he had been given to understand that he would be well advised to keep right out of it.

Suddenly, standing on the Boulevard, with thunder rumbling in the distance and the wind whirling clouds of dust along the sidewalks, he felt a longing to be there, an anonymous figure in the crowd, when the train left the station.

He nearly went back to ask the man at the undertaker's if he was sure that the baggage car was going to be attached to the passenger train.

Then he changed his mind. He did not have the courage to wait until five o'clock, or, above all, to see his in-laws getting into the train with the sewing machine and Jeanne's dresses.

He walked for a long time, without stopping to mop his forehead. The day before, he had walked like that, but today he had a destination in view.

Coming to the embankment, he followed it as far as Pont d'Austerlitz, where he spotted the modern building that housed what used to be called "the morgue" and was now the Medico-Legal Institute.

The façade suggested a business concern or a university building. A hearse of an unusual type was standing outside the door, with a chauffeur at the wheel. He saw nobody coming in or going out. They couldn't be coming for Jeanne's body yet, obviously, so perhaps they had brought someone else?

If he applied for permission, would they let him into the building, into the corridors at least? He hesitated. He had better not. Big drops of rain started to fall, bouncing off the surface of the Seine and pattering on the road.

Passers-by ran for shelter. Within a few moments, the sidewalks were shining and cars were beginning to splash water in all directions.

He smiled, not a happy smile, but one that Jeanne knew very well and that always intrigued her.

"What are you smiling for?" she used to ask.

"Nothing," he would answer.

"Anybody would think you were laughing at me."

"I've never laughed at you in my life."

"Then who are you laughing at?"

"Nobody."

He felt like taking off his hat to let the rain pour onto his head while he looked at the windows of the huge building one by one, like parents at the start of the school year trying to identify their child's classroom.

Jeanne was there, behind the walls, behind all those windows, but not for long now, because soon she would be going on a journey she had done once before, but the other way around.

"Are you happy, Bernard?"

It was that smile of his that invariably called forth this question from her.

"Why don't you answer me?"

"Because I don't know what to say."

"Then you aren't happy?"

"I'm not unhappy."

She pressed the point.

"But you aren't happy?"

He did not reply.

"Because of me?"

"No."

"You're sure?"

"Certain."

"You aren't sorry?"

"No."

On those days, a little later on, he would hear her sniveling in the next room. She would be trying to cry without making any noise.

Both of them had shown a great deal of patience. They had made a considerable effort, or, rather, a series of little efforts almost every day.

The policeman on traffic duty, whose oilskin was dripping wet, must be wondering what he was doing standing there, a great lanky figure, all by himself on the edge of the sidewalk, taking the rain without flinching. He could not be expected to guess that this, through the walls, was their last contact with one another. They had not been allowed any other. Besides, what good would it have done?

"Are you happy, Jeanne?"

She would smile at him quickly, a little too quickly. She was capable of putting a sparkle in her eyes from one second to the next.

"Why do you ask me that?"

"Because I'm not sure that I'm making you happy."

"You know very well that you're the kindest man in the whole world."

"No."

"With you, I'm happy."

With you! He had often thought about this. He had been watching her now for eight years. Some days, he thought he understood. At other times, he wondered whether, right from the start, he had not been on the wrong tack.

"You don't ever get bored?"

"Why should I get bored?"

He used to listen to them, her and Pierre, when they were both in the dining room and he was working in the studio. He could hear bursts of laughter and odd sentences which did not mean very much but which bubbled over with gaiety.

Some nights, lying alone in bed, she was seized with panic. He knew this because he had learned to recognize a certain way she had of tossing and turning, a certain rhythm in her breathing.

"Can't you sleep?"

"No."

He did not ask her why. It was he who went to get her a sleeping pill and a glass of water from the bathroom.

"Drink this."

"You aren't tired of me?"

He would stroke her hair.

"You will be one day. . . . It's bound to happen. . . . And then . . ."

The rain had soaked through his jacket, sticking his shirt to his skin, and his shoes were full of icy water.

He gave her a last look. The hearse stood motionless at the foot of the steps. A man came out, opened his umbrella, and started waving for a taxi.

He would have to go. There was no reason for him to stay there. He set off again, and had the courage to refrain from looking back. He was pleased with this squall that was swallowing him up and got back into his characteristic stride, by which he could be recognized from a distance.

"Even if I could see nothing but your legs, two hundred yards away . . ."

She watched him too, paying attention to his little habits, his idiosyncrasies, and particularly a slight quivering of his upper lip when he was prey to some emotion. Not necessarily a violent emotion. Or one with a profound or serious cause, either. On the contrary, it was nearly always aroused by something utterly trivial, an involuntary thought, a picture that came back to his mind, a word, the glance of a passer-by.

"What's wrong, Bernard?"

"Why should anything be wrong?"

"What are you thinking about?"

"I'm not even thinking."

She would search stubbornly, silently. This irritated him. He knew that, nine times out of ten, she would end up by finding out what she wanted to know, and, even if she said nothing of her discovery, he did not like being laid bare.

He had been right in his estimate of the moment when it would all begin. Now that he had finished with the body, with the funeral, the papers, the authorities, and the family, he found himself alone once more with her.

All of a sudden, he jumped onto a passing bus whose destination he had just noticed. The other passengers moved away from him, because he was soaked through. He tried to light a cigarette, but it went limp between his wet fingers.

It made no difference. He would find out, especially because he had not given up hope of recovering the letter. It was Saturday. The next day, Sunday, he would work on his sketch for *Art and Life*. He hoped that the rain would continue, for he enjoyed bending over his drawing board, next to the window looking out on the Boulevard, with the rain zigzagging down the windowpanes.

He was not going to eat again in a restaurant, not even at lunchtime today. He was going to resume his old habits, those he had before meeting Jeanne.

Ever since his first days in Paris, when he had accidentally discovered the apartment at Porte Saint-Denis, so dilapidated that nobody wanted it, he had made it a strict rule to cook his meals himself. In the morning, he used to go out and buy meat, ready-cooked vegetables, cheese, fruit, and sometimes a tart. When he got home, he would light the gas, fill the saucepans, and lay the table.

It was rare for him to leave dirty dishes lying around, and, at that time, he had a charwoman in for a half-day a week only. He probably would not be able to find her again. She was the widow of a military policeman and, if she was still alive, she would be too old to go out to work.

What was he going to say if Mademoiselle Couvert asked him again about the funeral? He did not want to shock her. Or the concierge, or anybody else. He had always tried to avoid shocking people.

He would tell them that his wife's family insisted on her being buried in her village. This was roughly the truth. Not entirely. Though, oddly enough, it had become the truth. The fact remained that he could still have brought Jeanne home if he had wanted to.

He went into the white shop of Madame Dorin, who had big, high breasts, almost under her chin. She gave him a dark look.

"Well now, Monsieur Jeantet, who would have believed it?"

He tried to model his expression on hers.

"Is it true that her parents arrived this morning? What a shock for the poor things!"

He might as well have done with it once and for all.

"They insisted on her being buried at Esnandes," he said very quickly.

"I can understand that. Not for anything in the world would I be buried in one of those modern cemeteries they're making around Paris. Where is it?"

"In Charente-Maritime."

"I thought she came from somewhere near Bayonne?"

"No."

"When is it?"

"Tomorrow."

"Are you leaving tonight?"

"I don't know yet. Will you give me a pound of butter, half a pound of kidney beans . . ."

He went on to the grocer's and the butcher's and, since he had no shopping bag, the wet parcels piled up in his arms.

The rain was coming down more heavily, in blinding gusts, the drops bouncing into the air, and the water in the gutters rising visibly along the sidewalks and spreading into the street. Claps of thunder exploded just above the rooftops and, in the half-light of the shops, women could be seen crossing themselves at every flash of lightning.

He went upstairs. On the landing, he had some difficulty in getting the key out of his pocket without dropping his bags. He managed it finally. He was home.

Putting everything down on the kitchen table, he began to shut the windows, for there were already several pools of water on the floor.

Then he took his jacket off and got down to his housework.

PART TWO

OTHER PEOPLE'S LIVES

1

His new life was not very different from the old, of which it had more or less retained the rhythm. He went on spending a certain number of hours every day at his drawing board, working slowly, for he was meticulous by nature, breaking off to sharpen his pencils, to clean his brushes and pens, to look out the window, or else because his eye was caught by an object, a stain, anything at all in the apartment.

Possibly he spent more time in his armchair than when Jeanne had been alive and, sitting there, lost track of the passage of time.

The days followed one another, to all appearances calm and empty. Anybody would have thought that he was leading a lazy life, for he was alone in his awareness of the subterranean processes going on within him.

Nothing happened. Outside events were insignificant and yet he paid careful attention to them, as if he were determined not to miss anything, as if everything counted. He sorted and classified in his head; often he went hunting through his memory for a comparison, a confrontation, a trifling incident in the past.

It was not a continuous monologue, a process of reasoning leading to logical conclusions. At the table, in his armchair, or in the streets, odd ideas occurred to him; he turned them over and over to consider them from every angle before putting them aside until a later date, like pieces in a jigsaw puzzle which would eventually find their place.

He was in no hurry. On the contrary, he was rather frightened, if anything, of finding out too soon.

He did his shopping, his cooking, his washing up. The shopkeepers grew accustomed to seeing him every morning at the same time, polite, self-effacing, waiting his turn, and looking vaguely at the counter, or at a quarter of beef hanging on a hook. He was perfectly aware that some of the women shoppers used to nudge each other and exchange glances behind his back, and that as soon as he went out tongues started wagging.

He had become a personality: the widower, the husband of the woman who had gone off to commit suicide in a hotel bedroom near the Champs-Elysées.

He could have avoided this curiosity. All that he would have had to do was to shop a couple of hundred yards farther on, to cross Boulevard Sébastopol, for instance.

That way he would have found himself in a different district, where nobody knew him.

The idea never occurred to him. He kept to his old habits, to a certain number of familiar faces. All his life, he had needed a routine, and it was only with the greatest reluctance that he resigned himself to changing from one to another.

To find a charwoman, he had had to go a long way up Faubourg Saint-Denis, asking concierges and shopkeepers, and climbing stairs up to the fifth or sixth floor a score of times. Women who were all over fifty and often seventy shook their heads: their time was fully occupied, or else they lived too far away and found it difficult to move about.

Madame Blanpain, the last to be approached, had agreed to come once a week, on Friday morning. She was middle-aged, as tall and broad-shouldered as he was, but tougher and sturdier. She lived with her daughter, who was preparing for the entrance examination at the Conservatoire.

She knew nothing about the suicide. The name Jeantet

had not reminded her of the paragraph that had appeared in the papers; no doubt she had not read it.

On her very first morning, she had started cleaning out the kitchen, then had set to work on the closets.

"I don't know who the lady was who lived here, and it's none of my business, but what I can say is that she wasn't very particular."

She had added, out of fear of having hurt him:

"Perhaps she went out to work and didn't have much time to give to the housework? . . ."

She found some hairpins and a broken comb in one closet, and even an old slipper, which Jeantet could not remember.

He had never noticed Jeanne's untidiness.

"If I could get a whole day clear next week, and if you agree, I could use it to wash the walls, because they really do need it. It would make the place a lot lighter."

She had done this. In order to clean the dining room, she was obliged to pull the folding bed from one corner into another. It was always getting in her way.

"Do you still use this old thing? Because it takes up such a lot of room. I know somebody in my building who's looking for a bed for a relative who's arrived from the provinces. If you didn't want too much for it . . ."

She had unpicked a few inches of a mattress seam, to find out what there was inside.

"It's wool. But it's a long time since it went through a carding machine. . . ."

A little old man had come for the bed with a handcart. This reminded him of the cart he had seen at the traffic light the Wednesday he had found the apartment empty, and that he had followed with his eyes for no particular reason.

This way pictures became jumbled together in his mind. He saw once more another handcart, one he had pushed himself, at Roubaix, when he was twelve years old and had gone to fetch a kitchen cupboard his mother had bought at an auction sale.

His brother had called him the first Sunday.

In the morning he was working, as he had decided to, by the window, and it was raining, not as heavily as the day before, but enough to trace liquid designs on the windowpanes. The ringing of the telephone had made him jump. He had thought of everything—of the police, of the undertaker's, of the railways—but not of his brother.

"This is Lucien speaking. I've seen the news in the paper. My wife and I would like to offer you our sympathy."

"Thank you, Lucien."

"How are you?"

"All right."

"We haven't had any notification and we wondered whether the funeral had already taken place. . . ."

That last sentence had been suggested to him by his wife.

"Her parents preferred to take the body back to their village."

"You aren't too depressed, I hope. Won't you come and see us one of these days?"

"Perhaps . . . Probably . . ."

"Blanche won't have heard the news, because she's on holiday at Divonne-les-Bains. You haven't seen anything of her lately, have you?"

"No."

"Nor have we. Her life is all very mysterious. If we happen to know that she's at Divonne, that's because she's sent the children a postcard. . . . Good-bye for now! . . ."

"Good-bye . . ."

Soon after marrying Jeanne, he had gone with her to see his brother and his sister-in-law, one Sunday, at their home at Alfortville. It was in December and, as Françoise said, you can't judge a house in winter, especially a sub-urban house. He had a recollection of rooms so small that you felt suffocated in them. The three children, at that time, were very young. The eldest must have been eight or nine and the youngest was still crawling about on the floor.

Lucien's wife had insisted on receiving them in the sit-ting room, which was obviously never used and where everything was fixed and lifeless. She had left them for a moment to rush around to a local pastry shop, and had given them tea. The children started crying. She got rid of them, except for the youngest, by sending them out to play, watching them through the window without stop-ping talking, or, to be more precise, asking questions.

Lucien, rather quiet and ill-at-ease, studied his brother and sister-in-law without giving any hint of what he was thinking.

"So you succeeded in persuading my brother-in-law to get married," said Françoise with feigned delight. "And he was always so scared of women before! How long have you known him?"

One question was followed by another. Where did you meet him? How did he set about proposing? Do you like children? How many would you like to have? . . .

Were you a salesgirl? A typist? No? What is your profession? Your parents let you go to Paris by yourself? You haven't any relatives there? You didn't have too hard a time to begin with?

That day, Jeantet discovered just how ill-natured his sister-in-law really was. Her light-hearted chatter did not quite manage to conceal a deliberate plan. She had made up her mind that she was going to know the truth, and he was convinced that after half an hour of this cruel game she had guessed everything.

Jeanne had lost her footing, trying to hold back her tears and casting imploring glances at him.

Lucien, for his part, did not bat an eyelid. He seemed to have bought peace for himself, once and for all, at the price of his silence.

Jeanne had remained thoroughly depressed for several days, and the memory of that day must have recurred to her at intervals. Long afterward, when they were talking together about relatives in general, she had asked him:

"Why didn't you dare tell yours the truth? Were you ashamed?"

He was not sure that she had believed him when he had assured her that it was not for his sake but for hers that he had kept silent. That was the truth. He was not ashamed of Jeanne's past.

"Admit that you're sometimes sorry. . . ."

"No."

He was perfectly sincere, and now that she was no longer there he realized this more than ever.

Several times, he had been on the point of saying to her, when they touched on this subject of the past:

"Don't you see that, on the contrary, it's precisely because of that . . ."

He stopped in time. It was difficult to explain, and even more difficult to understand. He himself was not sure that he understood.

He went to see Lucien the following Sunday, and found his brother thicker in the body, with his stomach bulging and his arms hairier than ever. His wife, who had dyed her hair red, had become extremely fussy about her appearance. They sat out in the little garden where Lucien used to grow vegetables and now there were only flowers to be seen.

"Marguerite and Jacques have gone for a swim. . . ."

Marguerite, the only daughter, would be thirteen now; Jacques was the boy who, the last time he had been there, was still wearing diapers.

"Julien is in the air force. He anticipated his call-up, so

that he could go into flying. He's an officer cadet in the training school at Saint-Raphaël."

Through the open window, he could see a modern living room, a model kitchen.

"The house has changed, hasn't it? It's a pity they've started building apartment houses opposite. It was almost like living in the country before, and you could see the Seine. Now we're always expecting to be bought up to make room for another housing scheme."

Lucien, looking at his brother and smoking his pipe, said:

"You haven't changed much. . . . How old are you in fact? . . . Thirty-nine?"

"Forty."

"Yes, of course, you were born in June."

He went off into the house to get some wine. His wife promptly seized the opportunity to ask:

"How did it happen? Did the police tell you all about it?"

He replied with a vague gesture.

"It must have been a shock to you, I'm sure. I always maintain, whatever Lucien says, that nothing happens that wasn't meant to happen, and that in the end we come to see that it was for our own good. In my opinion, if you'll allow me to say so, that woman wasn't normal. She wasn't made for you, or for your sort of life. That struck me the only time I saw her, and I said so afterward to your brother. She hadn't had an easy life, had she? You know, Bernard, you can't rub out the past however much you try."

Lucien came back with glasses and a bottle.

"What's that you were saying?"

"I was saying to Bernard that, all in all, it was a good thing for him. You remember that conversation we had eight years ago? What surprises me is that it lasted as long as it did. There was something in her eyes . . ."

Lucien glanced at his brother, afraid of seeing him looking hurt and angry, and was astonished to notice a smile on his lips.

"Well! Let's say no more about it. What's done is done! Are you happy in your work?"

"I've got a lot on my hands."

Because he had started work as an apprentice in a little printing shop at Roubaix, his family always pictured him in gray overalls in front of a press.

"I'm more or less my own boss. I work for magazines and publishing houses."

"Does that bring in much money?"

"Enough."

"You haven't been to see Mother?"

"No."

"We went at Christmas, with the children. She doesn't change. You'd be ready to swear that instead of growing older she was getting younger. It's old Poulard who's gradually fading away. When we were over there, he never left his armchair, and a neighbor used to come in every night to help Mother hoist him into bed. Young Méreau, you know, the fellow you went to school with, who owns a radio shop now. You remember Méreau?"

"A red-haired fellow?"

"Yes. He lives next door to the café, of which Mother will soon be the sole proprietor. To tell the truth, she's that already."

"I thought Poulard had a daughter?"

They were talking about their mother's second husband.

"She's still alive. She left her husband and her children to come to Paris."

"Then she'll inherit part of the estate at least?"

"Not the business, because Mother got Poulard to make it over to her as a gift *inter vivos*."

After that, they did not talk any more about Poulard or about Jeanne, but about him.

"You don't feel too lonely?"

"I'm getting used to it."

"Have you found somebody to do the housework?"

What was the point of admitting that he did it six days out of seven?

"Will you stay and have dinner with us? The children will be back soon. They can hardly remember you and they'll be delighted to meet their uncle at last."

"I have to get back to Paris. . . ."

He could not have said what use this visit had been to him, yet he felt quite sure that it had not been a waste of time.

Certain things his sister-in-law had said reminded him of Mademoiselle Couvert's remark:

"She didn't even try to be happy. . . ."

Jeanne had lived with him for eight years, in an area of a few square yards surrounded by walls and further isolated by a floor and a ceiling. But already he had some difficulty in visualizing her face, in picturing her figure in the places where she was in the habit of standing.

The picture remained hazy, did not seem true to life. He thought, for instance, of her black dress, of the whiteness of her skin, of her fair falling over one cheek, of her bare feet in a pair of slippers. She was sitting in front of her machine. Pierre came downstairs with his textbooks and his notebooks . . .

"May I come in, Monsieur Bernard? . . ."

From where he was sitting he could hear Jeanne and the boy talking, and the buzz of the sewing machine. Pierre was reading an arithmetic problem about some barrels of wine at so much a liter and some other barrels at so much. . . .

Jeanne appeared in the doorway, with a book in her hand.

"Have you got a minute to spare? Can you understand this problem?"

He could not manage to picture her as she was at moments such as that.

In the morning, she would come out of the bathroom naked; often there was something she had to see to on the gas stove before putting anything on. He knew the shape, the color, the consistency of her body, but at present that all seemed unreal to him.

She had not understood, the first time, when, one night, she had tried to slip into his bed, thinking that this would please him, and he had pushed her away. She had misinterpreted his reaction.

"Forgive me," she had stammered, picking up the pajama jacket he had lent her.

This was before the call paid by Inspector Gordes, of whose very existence Jeantet was unaware. The girl's cheek was a long way from being healed.

It must have been midnight. The lights were out and the studio was lit, intermittently, only by the neon sign of the clock shop.

He had put out his hand to grasp Jeanne's hand, and finally she had sat down on the edge of the couch.

"It isn't that," he had whispered.

She did not believe him, and tried hard not to cry, nonetheless, tears soon began trickling down her cheeks and one fell on the back of his hand.

"You're just saying that not to humiliate me. It was my fault. I'll leave here tomorrow. You've been kind to me and I ought to have understood right away. . . ."

But for that strange semidarkness, he would not have dared.

"Come closer . . ."

"You're just trying to be kind to me."

"No."

He whispered in her ear and, a few moments later, he could not be certain whether the tears moistening his cheek were Jeanne's or his own.

Avoiding words that were too specific, he tried to make her understand that he was not sure that he was capable, that it was for that reason that he had pushed her away, that he had never succeeded in possessing a woman completely.

Though he could not see her, he sensed on her part first amazement, then pity, and finally, later on, a sort of tenderness.

They were pressed close to one another.

"Have you really tried?"

"Yes."

"Often?"

"Fairly often."

He gathered that she was pointing in the direction of the hotel on the other side of the street.

"With . . . ?"

She too did not dare use specific words. After a silence, she went on, in a whisper:

"Ssh! . . . Don't talk any more . . . Leave it to me . . ."

He felt utterly ashamed. Time and again, he had tried to push her away. Never before had he felt so cut off from everything. Paris, the streets, the houses, the passers-by, the noises, all had ceased to exist. He was a body welded to another body. He could hear a different breathing from his own, and feel a heart beating that was not his own.

He felt like saying to her:

"What's the use, seeing that it's impossible?"

All the humiliations he had suffered came back to him, from a long way off, to pierce his heart.

If he could only put the light on, get back to reality, back to everyday life . . . But every time he moved, she hung on to him, saying:

"Ssh! . . ."

It was as if, little by little, she filled him with her will power, her self-assurance. Her body communicated to his its rhythm, its life.

At every fresh failure, he struggled to free himself, while she continued to treat it as a personal affair.

This went on for three hours, in the course of which he had the impression, a hundred times, of sinking into a dark and hopeless abyss, studded with gleams of light which went out as soon as he glimpsed them, the three most painful and most wonderful hours of his life.

He would never forget a woman's voice crying hoarsely, triumphantly:

"You see!"

He wept, this time from sheer happiness. She wept too, from fatigue and strain. She had just addressed him as *tu* for the first time, and she lay beside him, her cheek against his.

"Happy?"

Then, gently, with a tenderness he had never shown before, he had clasped her in his arms and, with a hand that hesitated in the dark, because of the painful scar, he had begun stroking her hair.

They had remained silent for a long time. Later, in a scarcely audible voice, he had murmured:

"You won't go away?"

She had squeezed his fingers, as if to seal a pact.

"You're sure you'll be able to live with me?"

"Yes."

"In spite of . . . ?"

She had laughed.

"You've got proof of that!"

"But . . ."

"Hush, now! . . . It's time you went to sleep. . . . You've got your work to do, tomorrow morning."

She had disengaged herself, and kissed him on the forehead, thoughtfully, as if that meant something in her eyes, and he had seen her pale body going toward the door.

In his mind, that was their night, the most important in

his life. In the morning, he did not dare to open his eyes. He could hear her going backward and forward in the narrow kitchen. She had put on her black dress, she had washed and done her hair, except for one lock, always the same one, which was hanging down over one cheek. She brought him his coffee, smiling timidly at him, as if she too were afraid that it would not last.

She very nearly addressed him as *vous*, which would have made things more difficult. Sensing this, she made an effort:

"Have you slept well?"

The worst part, the shameful part, the difficult part was over. Nothing remained but the best part, the triumphant cry of victory in the human warmth of the bed:

"You see!"

They had never spoken of it again, never. She recognized by certain signs, of which he himself was unaware, the nights when she could come to him. Perhaps it was on purpose that she hung around in her nightdress longer than usual? She said good night to him as she always did. As for him, he sometimes went on reading in his armchair for some time.

When at last he turned in, it was not long before he heard a creaking sound, the wire mattress of the folding bed. He never heard Jeanne's footsteps on the floor, but he knew even so that she was standing in the doorway, ready to beat a retreat if he failed to give the signal.

"Come here!"

That was their secret. At least, so he had thought. In the course of his visit, the previous Sunday, hadn't his sister-in-law said to him:

"It's a good thing you can't have any children. . . . When you think you might have been left with some kids on your hands! . . ."

Was it because of that that he had always looked hard

at the people with whom he came in contact, and even, sometimes, those he passed in the street?

When he had met Jeanne, he was quite resigned. At night, he sometimes stayed a long time at the window, watching what was happening on Rue Sainte-Apolline. He had not picked his apartment on purpose. He had come across it by chance, before he knew. Or at least, before he was sure.

It was the first hotel of that kind in Paris into which he had gone, with a woman, a blonde dressed in pink, and a quarter of an hour later he had come out, head down, swearing that he would never repeat the experiment.

Night after night, he saw the bedroom windows light up. The curtain of the left-hand window on the first floor did not close properly, and he could look straight down onto the bed.

Jeanne was to notice this later on, but only two or three months after they were married, for she rarely looked out on that side and then the bedroom had to be occupied. She had turned toward him, frowning, as if an idea had occurred to her, as if she had at last discovered the key to a mystery that had been worrying her.

The very first night, hadn't she had a suspicion of the same sort?

Now it became more specific. For her, he was no longer a stranger who had just picked her up in the street. She knew him better than anybody else in the world.

There had been, on that occasion, a moment of embarrassment between them. He would have liked to talk to her, to assure her that she was mistaken, that he had never spent an evening at that window, waiting for the light to go on in the bedroom opposite.

It had happened, admittedly, before Jeanne's time, because he still had hopes. In the end he would rush out of the apartment. He knew other streets, in other districts, with identical hotels and women pacing up and down in the half-light.

He too would stare them in the face, as he saw men doing outside his apartment. He did not bother about their looks, or about the shape of their bodies. He studied their eyes, their mouths, the expression on their faces. He had learned to recognize, at a glance, those who lost patience and those whose motherly pity froze his blood.

Was that what Jeanne had understood? Was it possible for anybody except himself to understand?

Even before he had become a widower, the people in the district used to look at him as if he were different from them, and he had often wondered if they guessed. He always had a feeling of suspicion and curiosity around him, as if people were trying to find out what was wrong with him.

Jeanne had come into his life by chance. He had no ulterior motive in going to pick her up from the sidewalk and he had been practically obliged to take her home with him.

He had planned nothing in advance. There had been their night, and, after that, he had built his life around her; she must have known that. She was his most precious possession. He wanted her to be happy. That was his chief preoccupation.

Not out of selfishness, to feel good and kind, or out of gratitude. He needed to know that one living creature in the world owed her happiness to him.

He wondered now whether she had understood. He was not sure. He himself was beginning to feel less certain than he had.

Every day, he did some work, sharpened his pencils, cleaned his pens and his brushes, did a little more work, and then, sitting in his armchair or eating by himself, he thought about Jeanne. He had the impression that she was becoming hazier, less important, and that it was really Bernard Jeantet that he was trying so hard to understand.

Perhaps it was not so much with her that he had lived for eight years as with himself? Hadn't she been just a presence, an accessory, or even an essential witness?

But a witness to what?

She had gone off to die, one afternoon, in a hotel bedroom of whose very existence he was unaware, in a different district from their own.

She had given her Boulevard Saint-Denis dress and her Boulevard Saint-Denis shoes to a chambermaid. They had found neither her handbag, nor her identity card, nor anything that came from him, that had some connection with him.

He had understood that right away, on Rue de Berry, and the flowers were a telltale sign, expressing, as it were, a desire for a complete change of environment. He had never given her any flowers. One day when she had brought some home from the market, he had been bad-tempered with her, and when she had asked him why, he had finally admitted that flowers irritated him.

It was true. He associated them with the countryside, which he disliked, and with suburban gardens fixed in sunny rigidity, like his brother Lucien's garden, the very sight of which filled him with an irrational panic.

Jeanne's death was a flight, and it was from him that she had fled.

He needed to know why. He had a right to know why. It was essential that he should, because the rest of his life depended on it, and that was the reason why he attached so much importance to the letter.

Even if she had written only a few lines, he would know how she had seen him, how he appeared in other people's eyes, in the eyes of somebody who had spent eight years watching him living.

At the *Art and Life* offices, Monsieur Radel-Prévost had waited two Wednesdays before saying to him, with a certain awkwardness:

"By the way, Jeantet, I've heard what's happened to you and would like to offer you my sympathy."

You could tell that he was wondering if he was right in doing so, that he was waiting for Jeantet's reaction.

"Thank you. That's very kind of you."

"You don't feel too lost? You're beginning to get over it?"

Then, absent-mindedly, looking at the photograph of his daughter, he added:

"I was going to ask you how you were managing about the children, but now I remember that you haven't any. . . . When are you taking your holidays this year?"

"I'm staying in Paris."

"Perhaps you're right, because there are crowds everywhere. . . . My wife and children are at Evian, and I'll be joining them there on Friday for three weeks. . . ."

Like this he saw Paris growing more and more deserted, and gaps appearing in the staffs of the firms for which he worked. Some offices closed down completely. Then he witnessed the opposite movement, beginning with the humblest employees and ending with the bosses, who continued to spend long weekends by the sea or in their country houses.

One Wednesday, after leaving Rue François-Premier, he walked along to Rue de Berry, without any definite plan in mind. He had always known that he would go back there. He stood for a long time on the sidewalk opposite the Hôtel Gardénia, and saw a couple go in. The woman was laughing. The man, who seemed very pleased with himself, looked rather like Monsieur Radel-Prévost.

He did not see the Italian maid. He tried to work out the time when she would come off duty.

He decided that he would come back another time.

He thought a great deal, that day, walking along the streets. And when he went to bed, though very tired, he lay for nearly two hours with his eyes open.

There was nobody there any more, in the doorway, to watch for his signal. . . .

2

One afternoon, about two o'clock, he had been surprised
to hear somebody walking up and down overhead. It was
not the boy playing. The footsteps were those of an adult,
occasionally moving around on the same spot, as when
Mademoiselle Couvert gave a customer a fitting, something that happened more and more rarely. Since her sight
had grown so much weaker, she had been given little new
work to do and did practically nothing but hemming and
mending.

Later on, he had recognized the old woman's hesitant
step on the stairs and, a quarter of an hour after that, looking out of the window, he had seen her waiting for a bus
on the other side of the Boulevard.

She had put on her Sunday best, with gloves, a hat, and
shoes, which she scarcely ever wore and which made her
ankles bulge.

Why had this outing of the dressmaker's preoccupied
him? She might have had some relatives to visit, a sick
friend, a small pension to collect. For all that they had
lived in the same building for such a long time, he knew
practically nothing about her.

Ever since Jeanne's death, Pierre had avoided him. He
had not been to see him once, and when they passed on
the stairs, the boy would start running as if he were suddenly in a hurry.

He did not see the old woman come home. That evening, he knew that she was back from the characteristic shuffling noise of her felt slippers.

Once when she had heard that noise, as soft as the beating of a pair of wings, Jeanne had smiled and said:

"Our good angel is going to bed!"

He suspected the existence of an intimacy between her, Mademoiselle Couvert, and the boy, in which he had not been invited to share, and when Jeanne came down from the third floor, where she used to spend long periods, she never told him what they had been talking about.

In the rambling conversations, too, between her and Pierre, he noticed allusions to subjects which remained a closed book to him. He had not worried about this at the time. He knew nothing about children. They rather frightened him, not so much as animals, but in the same way, perhaps for the same reasons, and he tended to keep them at a distance.

The day after Mademoiselle Couvert's outing, a more normal event occurred. Shortly before four o'clock, the door opened on the fourth floor, and somebody started coming downstairs. It was impossible to confuse the old woman's footsteps with those of any other tenant. Since her sight had become poor, she paused after every two steps, hesitating, with one hand grasping the banister and the other feeling the wall.

It was a steep staircase, with bends where the steps, on one side, came to a point. Another old woman, who used to live on the fifth floor with a husband of the same age, had broken a hip falling down it. She had not died as a result, but she had spent over a year in plaster, and they had never seen her again, because the authorities had sent her to an old people's home.

He heard Mademoiselle Couvert come down her two steps, stop, then come down two more. Then, when she had got to the landing, outside his door, he heard nothing more.

118

This seemed to him to last an eternity. She did not go down any farther. She did not knock either. He was beginning to lose patience, wondering whether she had fainted, when he heard her set off again, this time back upstairs.

He went to the door, opened it, and caught a glimpse of a dark skirt disappearing around the bend in the stairs.

It was Thursday. He had to wait till Friday, at about the same time, to get the solution to the riddle. He was in his armchair this time when he heard her come down and, like the day before, stop outside his door. After a more or less prolonged wait in the dark, was she going to go upstairs again?

The silence lasted for half a minute and then, at last, there was a knock at the door.

He opened the door right away and was struck by the old woman's solemnity. Her face, which was naturally pale, wore the expression of somebody who is ready to take an important step, and her clothes were a compromise between those she had put on two days before to go into town and the more ordinary clothes he was used to seeing her wearing at home.

"I'm not disturbing you, am I?"

With something akin to suspicion, she looked past him to make sure that he was alone.

"Not at all. Do come in."

He pointed to his armchair, which was still warm, but she shook her head.

"It's too low for me. I prefer an upright chair."

She inspected the white walls, the drawings, the brushes standing in their glasses, and then, surreptitiously, glanced through the half-open door into the dining room, which had been Jeanne's domain for so long.

She must have known this, must have been acquainted, at second hand, with all the details of the apartment, and no doubt the details of their life together too. Perhaps she had been here before, in his absence?

She said nothing, but folded her hands in her lap, which seemed to suggest that she was going to be there for some time to come. A hidden mechanism slowly warmed up, then finally started, and her colorless lips began moving.

"I haven't come here for the fun of it, I can tell you that. . . ."

She had chosen to fix her eyes on the window. She paused for a moment, as if she still hoped that he might help her by asking questions.

"You can't guess what I've come about?"

"No."

"Then she was right."

"Are you talking about Jeanne?"

He could sense no sympathy for him in her: on the contrary. You might even have said that she was shocked to hear him referring familiarly to the dead woman.

"If it wasn't that I've got fewer and fewer customers on account of my eyes, and that school will be starting again soon . . ."

He guessed that it was a question of money, though he was still a long way from the truth. Yet during Jeanne's lifetime he had sometimes asked himself certain questions, out of the blue, thinking as he did about so many things.

"He's grown some more this summer, and I'll have to fit him out again from head to foot. . . ."

He had before him a statue, a monolith. She did not move a muscle. Her skin scarcely quivered. Only her lips moved now and then, after long silences during which her eyes remained fixed in a glassy stare.

"Now that she isn't here any more to do the necessary . . ."

He thought he understood.

"You mean that Jeanne helped you?"

He was not surprised. There was one thing that puzzled

him, however: he wondered where Jeanne had got the money.

"Of course! It was only natural that she should pay me his keep. . . ."

She looked at him with a hard, defiant gaze.

"I'd have preferred to go on bringing him up by myself, I can tell you that, and I haven't come here because I like it. . . ."

"Then Pierre is . . . ?"

"Any woman would have understood right away. If you hadn't been so taken up with yourself, like all men are, you'd have understood too. . . . It wasn't you I wanted to ask, but Monsieur Jacques. . . . I went to see the police, over there on Rue de Berry, where they've been dealing with her case, and I tried to get his name and address. . . . But they refused to let me have them. . . ."

That was why, two days before, she had put on her best dress and waited for the bus at the corner of the Boulevard.

"I even went to the Hôtel Gardénia. They were very polite there, but they told me it was against the rules to communicate patrons' addresses. If only she'd told me, before going off like that, what she wanted me to do!"

Pierrot was nearly ten. That meant that he was eighteen months old when Jeanne had come into Jeantet's life. She had never spoken to him about a child. She had waited until he was six years old, until he had reached school age, before lodging him with the old woman, in the same building.

"I wonder why she never told me," he murmured.

In a voice filled with something like hatred, she replied:

"Because she regarded you as a sort of god and she lived in deadly fear of disappointing you or hurting you! In her eyes you weren't like other men, and you knew it; you did everything you could to make sure that she went on seeing you that way. Would you have taken the child in?"

He did not know what to reply. He wondered whether he would willingly have accepted the presence of a third person in his apartment, with all the complications involved. He would have been incapable, for instance, of living like his brother, Lucien. It is true that that was a different matter.

Honestly, he didn't know.

"She knew you pretty well, didn't she? Besides, she didn't want the boy to know that she was his mother. They all have the same idea. They make up all sorts of stories, even if it lands them in a mess. . . ."

"Does he still not know?"

"I told him the truth last week."

"Why?"

"Because I saw that he had his suspicions and I didn't want him to worry his little head about it."

"What else did you tell him?"

"Everything."

She spoke more defiantly than ever, as a woman conscious of doing her duty.

"Don't you imagine that children don't know a lot more than people think, especially in a district like this! I explained that he was born before she met you, and that she had never dared to talk to you about it. . . ."

"Where was he born?"

"At the Maternité, Boulevard de Port-Royal."

The hospital where his sister Blanche worked! Blanche had perhaps had Jeanne in her ward, looked after her, even—who knows?—shown the mother the newborn baby.

He did not dare to ask all the questions that occurred to him and felt sorry that he had to get the answers out of this hostile old woman.

"Was she living by herself at the time?"

"You're very inquisitive all of a sudden, now that it's too late! Perhaps if you'd shown a little interest in her before, nothing would have happened. . . ."

"What do you mean?"

"Do you think it's human to take a woman and then decide, from one day to the next, that she hasn't got a past?"

Jeantet's face turned red, as it had done at the police station that first evening, when it had seemed to him that Gordes and he were speaking different languages.

He had just been accused of making Jeanne unhappy, of being the cause of her death, when in fact, if he had kept quiet for years, that had simply been for her sake.

But was he really sure? The old woman, with her calm, stern gaze, was giving him doubts about everything.

"She was living with a man, of course, and earning her living near the Montparnasse station, just as later she tried earning it here. . . ."

She glanced briefly at the hotel opposite.

"She'd sent out the child to nurse, not far from Paris, toward Versailles. That cost a lot, because those people take advantage of you. The man insisted on her handing the child over to the Board of Guardians. She decided that, if she was on her own, she could keep all she earned and then she'd have enough to pay for her son.

"She went off one night, thinking that once she'd changed her district he wouldn't find her. She'd even left him a letter telling him she was going back to the country, that it was no use looking for her, and that she'd never live with him again. . . ."

"Was it she who told you all that?"

"Who else would it have been? Do you think that she didn't know what she'd done, or that those are things you must forget?"

Would Jeanne have talked to him too if he had asked her questions or if he had put her in the right mood for confidences?

She had thought that he refused to know, that he wanted to take her without her past.

"It took him only three days to find her, and then he punished her by marking her. . . ."

So the woman he had taken in was a different Jeanne from the one he had imagined. He too had spoken another language with her, making their conversation pointless.

"When did she take you into her confidence?"

"When she decided to have her son near her."

"Then before that, she didn't see him?"

"Once a week, on Wednesday of course. She had to take a taxi, which cost her a lot, and be quick about it."

The Wednesday afternoons that he devoted to what he called his rounds . . . Rue François-Premier, then the Faubourg Saint-Honoré and Monsieur Charles at the end of the corridor, with his indigestion pills, and finally the *Stock Exchange Press* and the men in gray work coats working all around him . . . That day, for Jeanne, had a different meaning. . . . She had to find time to dress, to go over there, sitting nervously in her taxi, to come back, and to resume a familiar pose in the flat. . . .

If Jeantet's life, his routine, his movements had not been as carefully calculated as if he had been the crank he nearly was, all this would have been impossible. He would have arrived home at least once before he was expected, and not found her in the apartment or in the local shops, where he would probably have gone looking for her.

He could not quite believe it, and put forward an objection.

"But what about the money?"

"Oh, yes, it's time we came to the money! Your stinginess made things difficult for her and no mistake!"

The accusation was false. He was not stingy, or miserly either. The proof of that was that he could have earned a lot more by accepting work he did not like. At *Art and Life*, he had been offered a job with a salary, which would have relieved him of all financial worry. He could have obtained a well-paid job at the *Stock Exchange Press* too, and in at least two publishing houses.

He had preferred his freedom, the solitude of his studio, the somewhat free-and-easy life he led, in constant contact with Jeanne, in the snug little world of their apartment.

But that world had existed only in his imagination, and now he was being told that he had been tight-fisted with his money.

"I gave her . . ."

"You gave her, every morning, the money she asked for to do her shopping."

"Well?"

It happened to be out of prudence that he used to put in a drawer the money he brought home every Wednesday evening. The drawer was not locked. She could have taken what she needed out of it.

When, at the beginning, he had brought her something to wear, she had looked sad and upset.

"I always seem to be asking you for something. I just make your life difficult. . . ."

She used to bring him back the change, and made it a point of honor to give an account of what she had spent.

"This morning, I paid the baker's bill, and the butcher's cost me four hundred and fifty-three francs. . . ."

It was not he who had imposed this routine on her. He had only accepted it, out of tact. She was afraid of appearing to be grasping, and he thought he could understand why. She bought only the cheapest things for herself, and if she took no care over her appearance, that was deliberate.

He had told her:

"I love you as you are, in your black dress, with that lock of hair falling over one cheek, and your rather pale lips. . . ."

It was not because make-up would have reminded him

of the past. They had misunderstood each other, in all good faith.

And now an old maid who had never been in love was setting herself up as a judge, taking up the cudgels for Jeanne and speaking, as it were, in her name, accusing him of a sort of perverseness.

"She was obliged to cheat. . . . A few francs here . . . A few francs at the grocer's . . . Then, when Pierre had to go to the hospital to have his appendix out . . ."

He had never heard anything about this, and gazed anxiously at the old woman, wondering what else was going to come out of her pale, cruel mouth.

"That was before I took him in. . . . He was still living in the country. . . . She didn't want them to put him in a public ward. . . . I forget how much it cost her, but it was a tidy sum. . . ."

They had lived all that time a few feet apart, only rarely spending an hour without looking at one another or speaking to one another, and yet she had been thinking of all these different matters, solving problems of which he had no inkling.

"How did she manage?"

"Can't you guess? I'd just been taking in a dress for a customer who'd grown thinner, a silk dress it was, with blue flowers on it. I could still see all right at that time. She tried it on. The dress fitted her as if it had been made for her. She asked me to lend it to her for an afternoon. She went to Rue Caumartin. . . ."

On a Wednesday!

"It seems there's a chic little bar there, next door to a hotel. In a couple of hours, she earned enough to pay the hospital costs."

"Did she go back there?"

"What difference does it make whether she went there once, or ten times, or a hundred times? Come to that, what difference does it make whether she went there at all? Didn't you know about her when you asked her to stay with you? Did she lie to you?"

She was talking like Inspector Gordes. She too could have said:

"One in a thousand . . . *And even then!*"

"Well, there you are. Now you know. If it hadn't been for the boy, who can't help it, I wouldn't have come down here and I'd have left you with your convenient ideas. . . ."

. . . *convenient ideas* . . .

Quite honestly, he wondered if he deserved such harsh condemnation.

"Go on . . ."

"What do you want to know?"

"Everything."

"You haven't heard enough?"

"I need to understand."

"There's nothing difficult to understand. She was obliged to do now and then what she used to do every day. She wasn't robbing you of anything. But because men have their own ideas, she had the courage to keep it all to herself, to cheat, to lie, to leave you to your smugness. . . ."

Smugness! . . .

He had always taken the dressmaker for a rather dim, stupid old maid; now, all of a sudden, he began to think that she knew things about him that he had never suspected. Out of sheer spite, she was taking a malicious pleasure in distorting them.

"If I'd had the choice, I'd have preferred to do the same as she did and talk to Monsieur Jacques rather than to you. . . ."

He had to swallow his saliva before asking:

"Did he know?"

"Know what?"

"About the boy? . . ."

"For the last year, he was the one who paid for his keep."

"Where did he meet her?"

He was beginning to be afraid that the man had actually come to his own apartment.

"Why, on Rue Caumartin!"

"A long time ago?"

"Just over a year ago, as I've already told you . . ."

"Did she go back after that?"

"Back where?"

"To Rue Caumartin . . ."

"Why should she, seeing that he took care of everything? He kept pressing her to leave you too. He rented a room for her by the month and bought her dresses and underwear that she hardly ever had a chance of wearing. . . ."

Always on Wednesday afternoon! He passed quite close to Rue de Berry on his way from Rue François-Premier to Faubourg Saint-Honoré.

"Do you know what he's like?"

"Oh, yes, a real gentleman. He's in business, he's got a big yellow car, and he lives over by the Bois de Boulogne."

"Is he married?"

"Of course."

"Any children?"

"Two. It was the children that prevented him from getting a divorce. Because it was he who was in the wrong, the court would have given custody of the children to his wife, and he didn't want to be separated from them. . . ."

"Would Jeanne have asked for a divorce?"

"She didn't tell me. I don't think so, but I'd have backed her up if she had."

He was no longer as sure as he had been that the letter was meant for him. Wasn't it because the envelope bore another address that the police had told him there hadn't been a letter in the bedroom?

He would find out. That was still absolutely essential. He had come out of the fog now and he would not go on asking his questions in the same way. They had been unable to understand him, and that was natural, but they would be dealing with a different man from now on.

For a moment, though he was still rather overwhelmed, he knew that he would get over it, that he would eventually be able to look the facts in the face. He had already practically forgiven Mademoiselle Couvert, who had not unfolded her hands once during the whole conversation.

"Well, about the boy, what have you decided?"

"Does he know that you've come to see me?"

"No. I took care to send him to the movies. Yesterday too, because I came downstairs yesterday afternoon. At the last moment . . ."

"Why haven't you spoken to him about it?"

"Because there was a danger that he might not agree."

"He doesn't like me?"

"Before, he was just jealous . . ."

"But he didn't know that Jeanne was his mother. . . ."

"What of it? Does that prevent a child from being jealous? After what has happened, he hates you."

"You mean he thinks it's my fault?"

"If it isn't your fault, whose fault is it?"

He was not in a mood to defend himself. He would have done it clumsily and run the risk of getting into even deeper waters.

"If you tell me what my wife used to pay you, I'll give you the same amount every month. . . ."

"That won't be enough, now that he's grown such a lot and everything is so much dearer, clothes, shirts, and especially shoes. . . ."

"I'll pay you whatever sum you want."

She was taken aback by such an easy victory, as Jeanne's parents, at the town hall, had been by theirs. She began looking at him with new interest, not unmixed with suspicion.

She nonetheless offered an apology of sorts.

"It wasn't for the fun of it that I came and told you all this. As soon as I started asking you for the money, I had to tell you the whole story. . . ."

"You did right."

"You don't bear her a grudge?"

"Jeanne?"

"Yes, of course. Because you'd be wrong if you did. If she hadn't bothered so much about you . . ."

The worst of it was that he had a vague feeling that she was right.

"A woman can't live at the end of a leash. . . ."

He suddenly saw Jeanne, more clearly than at any time during the last few weeks, in the dining room, in front of her sewing machine, in the kitchen, in the doorway waiting for a sign from him.

Hadn't she lived in the apartment for eight years like a pet animal that goes from one corner to another, paying careful attention to its master's mood, and waiting hopefully for a pat on the head or a kind word?

"I do so want you to be happy!"

The queer thing was that he used to say and think the same thing. Didn't it annoy her, in the end, to feel him watching her anxiously? Knowing what his reply would be, she used to ask him:

"What are you thinking about?"

"You."

"And what are you thinking?"

"I'd like to be sure that you are happy. . . ."

She would pretend to laugh, or else she would come and kiss him on the forehead. Had that ever happened on a Wednesday evening? Probably. And, a little earlier, she had been to Rue Caumartin to earn her son's keep, or, later on, Rue de Berry, to meet the man she called "Monsieur Jacques" when she talked about him to Mademoiselle Couvert.

Because she talked about him to her. She felt the need

to talk to somebody. Not to him. To the old woman on the floor above.

She talked about Jeantet too, saying simply:

"He's so kind!"

Didn't she realize that he wasn't kind, that he was just a man?

What would have happened if she had told him the truth? He hadn't the slightest idea. He had just learned too much of the truth, all at once. What was certain was that his instinct hadn't deceived him. Time and again he had been a prey to an uneasy feeling, an impression of unreality, inconsistency.

He shut himself up between these walls, and shut Jeanne up with him, to convince himself that the two of them existed, that they formed a whole, that their life was a real life. As an extra precaution, he insisted on things being in their allotted places, as if they had their part to play too, and on every hour of every day being filled in exactly the same way. Like that, he naïvely imagined that there could not be any leakage.

In this way, holding his breath all the time, he had built up an imaginary existence, which the old woman had just blown at as she would at a candle.

"For the month that's just over . . ."

"I beg your pardon. How much is it?"

"With the clothes I've got to buy him, the books he'll need at the beginning of school . . ."

She counted under her breath, then stated a figure, watching him to see whether he thought she was asking too much.

"Jeanne knew that I asked her for only the absolute minimum. . . ."

He did not argue, but opened the drawer, the money drawer, which, after the old woman's accusations, had taken on a different aspect. He counted out the notes.

"Thank you for the boy's sake. If I manage to find Monsieur Jacques's address, I won't come and bother you again."

"There's no need for you to look for it."

"You mean you'll go on paying?"

He nodded, and accompanied her to the door, pulling aside the chair she was on the point of bumping into. She did not look around, but started climbing the stairs with her hesitant walk.

He shut the door, a gesture that no longer had the same meaning as before. For years, that had been for him a symbolic gesture, a sort of rite, a kind of exorcism. He would cross the yard, where the concierge's lamp could be seen burning behind the dirty windowpane, open the door without needing to use his key, and hear Jeanne get up from her chair in one of the rooms. Even if she did not move, he knew that she was there, he could feel her presence, and then shutting the door was like putting a barrier between them and everything that was dangerous, hostile, menacing.

They remained alone between these walls, with nothing but the anonymous noises they were willing to admit, and a bird's-eye view of the roofs of buses and scurrying passers-by who could do nothing to harm them.

What he thought just then, what he felt in his heart of hearts, he had never explained to Jeanne. He had never thought about it at all clearly. And only once, sinking into his armchair and stretching his legs, he had sighed:

"It's good to be home!"

Weren't his gestures expressive enough, his way of coming into the studio, of hanging up his hat, of looking at the two drawing boards, the letters in India ink, and Jeanne as she broke off from her sewing or her cooking?

When he was a boy, at Roubaix, there was a bank clerk who always went to work and came home at exactly the same time, to the very minute. They used to see him walking along the opposite sidewalk and, twenty yards from his front door, he had already taken his key, at the end of a shining chain, out of his jacket.

He took long strides too, almost as slow as Jeantet's, which gave a touch of solemnity to his walk. He held his head high, and wore an impassive expression of unvarying serenity, so that more than once the boy had heard his mother say:

"You'd think he was carrying the Blessed Sacrament. . . ."

Perhaps Jeanne thought that he too looked as if he were carrying the Blessed Sacrament? Hadn't Mademoiselle Couvert said just now, with an impatience tinged with malice, that his wife regarded him as a sort of god?

God had flopped into his armchair. As it happened, the bank clerk himself, one evening when he was coming home from the office and already had his key in his hand, had collapsed on the sidewalk only a few yards from his front door.

There was a sound of footsteps running upstairs, a door banging on the floor above. Pierre had come home from the movies, and the first thing he had done was probably look in the oven to see what there was for dinner.

Jeantet, who was staring at the wall, at one of the letters of his unfinished alphabet, the Jeantet alphabet, which he had been working on for years, suddenly shut his eyes, because his eyelids were prickling.

There was no anger in him, no rancor, possibly even no bitterness. His fingers opened gently, closed on nothingness, opened again, and began stroking, tenderly and awkwardly, the leather of his old armchair.

3

He had not come, this time, as an ordinary petitioner, and he accorded only a casual glance to the people waiting on the bench, with their backs against a wall covered with official posters. He went up to the counter and spoke to the duty sergeant, who was listening to a quietly dressed woman telling him with tears in her eyes how a young hooligan—"a child, officer! I'm positive he wasn't more than fourteen!"—had snatched her bag from her hands on the Grands Boulevards.

"I have an appointment with Inspector Gordes," he said, interrupting this monologue.

"He's expecting you. You can go right up. You know the way?"

He had taken the precaution of telephoning to Gordes, who had not appeared to be surprised. In the first room, where two men were typing and there was an Algerian waiting on a chair, they pointed to the Inspector's door, which he remembered perfectly well.

"Knock on that door. And don't be afraid of knocking hard, because he'll have his window open."

Gordes had taken off his jacket, and there was a half-empty glass of beer on his desk.

"Come in, Jeantet. I always thought we'd meet again."

He made no secret of examining him with a visible curiosity, any more than he concealed his surprise at the change that had occurred in his attitude.

Jeantet took this as a tribute, for he himself had the feeling that at last he had left his childhood behind him. He was still rather timid. To be more precise, he was suffering from a certain awkwardness, a lack of practice, and his eyes hesitated to look people in the face.

The mere fact that he had telephoned was significant and, seeing that Gordes was not asking him any questions, he went straight to the point.

"I've come to ask you to do me a service, to give me a piece of information that I need and that it's easy for you to get hold of, whereas it's almost impossible for me."

There was irony, but not spiteful or aggressive irony, in the policeman's eyes.

"It's about a name and an address. You see what I'm getting at?"

This time, Gordes frowned as he pressed down the tobacco in his pipe with a stained forefinger.

Jeantet went on:

"I know that his Christian name is Jacques. At the Le Roule police station, they won't tell me anything, and the hotel hasn't the right to give its patrons' addresses."

"You've been and asked?"

"I haven't. Somebody else."

"On your behalf?"

"No."

"Perhaps if you told me . . ."

"An old maid who lives on the floor above mine, and who's been boarding my wife's son for some years . . ."

Gordes scratched his nose.

"So she had a son?"

"I found out only three days ago."

"Born before you came along?"

"Yes. Ten years ago. When I met his mother, he was out for nursing. Didn't you know?"

"I didn't pursue my inquiries as far as that. It was a very ordinary case. Nobody had lodged a complaint. What I don't understand is why you want that name and address. I just don't see the connection with the child."

"There isn't any connection."

"Well, then?"

"I must see the man."

"Does he know of the boy's existence?"

"He's never seen him. But he's been paying for his keep for the past year."

Gordes chewed the stem of his pipe with a certain satisfaction in his eyes, but a good deal of curiosity too.

"How did you find all that out? Was it the old woman who opened your eyes?"

"Yes. She couldn't get hold of the address either, and she needed some money."

"So she came and asked you for it, eh? And spilled the beans! But when I told you a tenth part, a hundredth part of the truth, you refused to believe me."

"I'm sorry."

"And what do you want to do with this gentleman?"

"See him, talk to him."

"What about?"

"I think that the letter was intended for him."

"So you still believe in the existence of that ghost letter?"

"I know that your colleagues will go on denying it, but I'm convinced that Jeanne wrote a letter."

"And you want to know what she wrote to another man?"

Perhaps he was beginning to think that Jeantet had not developed as much as he had thought at first? He was still looking at him with curiosity, but it was more the professional curiosity of somebody adding a rare specimen to his collection.

"Why is it me that you've come to see?"

Jeantet did not dare to tell the truth. He had thought that the Inspector would do him this service out of conceit, to show him that everything was easy for him, that his powers were greater than people imagined, and also out of curiosity, in order to know how the story ended.

"The first time you came to see me, you didn't believe me and you regarded me as a brute trying to desecrate something sacred."

"But you'll do this for me just the same?"

"Are you armed?"

"I've never owned a revolver in my life, and I wouldn't know how to use one."

"You swear you won't do anything stupid?"

"I swear."

"In that case, come back and see me tomorrow at the same time."

At the door, he asked a final question.

"Did you give the old woman some money?"

"Yes."

"I'll see you tomorrow, then."

Jeantet was convinced that he no longer walked in the same way, that he had the courage now to look passers-by in the face, and that his big body had acquired greater consistency, greater weight. Wasn't even the woman at the dairy conscious of the change and didn't she follow him with astonished eyes when he went out of her shop?

He kept his appointment the next day. Once again, he was told to go upstairs right away, but he had to wait in the first room for a quarter of an hour, because Gordes was questioning a shoplifter. He saw her when she came out. She looked rather like his charwoman, Madame Blanpain, and she was so massive that for a moment he took her for a man in disguise.

"Come in, Jeantet . . . Sorry to keep you waiting . . ."

He sat down on the chair, which was still warm, and lit a cigarette, a significant action, because he would not have taken this liberty a week before. The window was open, looking out on a courtyard in which there were two police trucks, one of which, occupied by six men with guns, was ready to go. There was probably a fight going on somewhere or other, or else a political gathering.

"You remember what you promised me?"

He nodded.

Gordes had a slip of paper in his hand and was playing with it.

"Don't take my next question the wrong way. This man is married and occupies a prominent position. I suppose you aren't thinking of kicking up a scandal?"

"I want to ask him for an appointment, and I'm ready to meet him wherever he likes—here, if you insist."

"There is no question of that. He lives in Neuilly; the address doesn't matter, because it isn't to his home that you'll have to write or telephone. I don't know if his wife is jealous and keeps a sharp eye on him. You can never take too many precautions."

Jeantet nodded approvingly.

His name is Beaudoin, Jacques Beaudoin, and he's a northerner, a native of Lille, unless I'm mistaken."

"I come from Roubaix."

"I know. You're neighbors, so to speak. He runs a big electronic-equipment business, the SANEC, which does national-defense work, so he's known in all the ministries. He's got factories in various parts of France, he travels abroad a lot, especially in the States, and he got back from Boston a week ago."

"He was there when . . . ?"

"Yes. He knows all about it though. My colleague Massombre has been to see him at his office."

"Did they talk about me?"

"Massombre didn't tell me."

"You still don't know anything about the letter?"

"They all swear there isn't a letter. You still refuse to believe them?"

"Yes."

138

"Well, that's your business. If you have the opportunity, come and see me afterward. Unless you'd rather I dropped in on you one of these days."

"You'd be very welcome."

Wasn't this already a lot more tangible, more real? His fingers did not tremble when, in his apartment, he picked up the telephone and dialed a number. The SANEC offices were on Rue Marbeuf, a stone's throw from Rue François-Premier, a stone's throw too from Rue de Berry.

"This is SANEC. Who do you want to speak to?"

"Monsieur Jacques Beaudoin, please."

"Who's speaking?"

"Bernard Jeantet."

"Monsieur Beaudoin is in conference and can't be disturbed before eleven o'clock."

It was ten o'clock. He did not try to work to kill the time. He went and planted himself in front of the window, then sat down in his armchair, listening for some time to Pierrot, who had obviously invented a new game and was coming and going overhead, pulling some heavy object behind him.

At eleven o'clock precisely, he once again dialed the Rue Marbeuf number and heard the same young, pleasantly modulated voice.

"This is Bernard Jeantet . . ."

"Just a moment, please . . . I'll see if the conference is over.'

This took a long time. He thought that he had been cut off and he was on the point of hanging up when at last another woman's voice said:

"This is Monsieur Jacques Beaudoin's office. Who is asking for him?"

He repeated, with a somewhat derisive smile:

"Bernard Jeantet."

Were they trying to overawe him by giving so much importance to the other man? After all, he was only

Jeanne's husband, the widower now, a queer character they had never seen.

"I'll put you through to Monsieur Beaudoin."

Somebody coughed at the other end of the line.

"Hello. Who's speaking?"

He repeated his name for the third time at least, knowing that the other knew perfectly well who was calling:

"Bernard Jeantet."

"Yes . . . Go ahead . . ."

"I should like to meet you. I called to ask you where and when it would be possible."

During the silence that followed, he could distinctly hear the sound of rather heavy breathing.

"I suppose you can't give me the message over the telephone?"

"It isn't a message."

"I'm very busy at the moment."

"I know. It won't take long."

"Listen . . . In my office, it's difficult. . . . Hang on a moment . . . I'm thinking. . . . Do you know the Plaza bar?"

"The Hôtel Plaza, on Avenue Montaigne?"

"That's right. . . . The bar is in the basement. . . . About three o'clock or half past three, there's nobody there. . . . How about this afternoon at three? . . . One moment while I look at my engagement book . . ."

He was not alone in his office, and Jeantet could hear him speaking, presumably to his secretary. He said to her, without thinking of putting his hand over the receiver:

"Anyway, it won't take long. . . . I've no intention of allowing myself to be led by the nose. . . . Call the Morton brothers, to put off their appointment till four . . . Half past four, to be safer . . . Hello, Monsieur Jeantet? . . . It's agreed then, for this afternoon at three, in the Plaza bar. . . . Just ask the barman for me."

He had the feeling that he had made more headway in

two days than in the weeks since Jeanne had died. Everything tied up, without a single hitch. He had not even had to change his habits. He had time to cook his meal, have lunch, wash up and tidy the kitchen, and finally wash himself and put on a clean shirt.

At the corner of the Boulevard he caught the same bus as old Mademoiselle Couvert when she had gone to the police station in the Eighth Arrondissement, got off at the Rond-Point des Champs-Elysées, and slowed down on Avenue Montaigne because he was a quarter of an hour early.

He was smoking a lot. This was the only change in his habits in the last three days. He had stopped counting his cigarettes, and sometimes he lit one from another.

He was not annoyed that Monsieur Jacques, as he went on calling him in his mind, had chosen the bar of a palatial hotel for their appointment. It was not necessarily to disconcert him, but because he had thought that they would not be disturbed there.

In the lobby, a man in a gray frock coat, with a silver chain around his neck and white gloves, asked him politely but firmly:

"What are you looking for, Monsieur?"

"The bar."

"It is closed just now."

"I have an appointment there with Monsieur Jacques Beaudoin."

"At the end of the hall, the staircase on the left . . . I haven't seen Monsieur Beaudoin come in yet."

He went past the showcases framed in gilded metal, followed the wrought-iron banisters, turned the wrong way, caught a glimpse of some women in a hairdressing salon, and finally came to a big room that was dark and cool, with a low ceiling and deep leather armchairs.

He could see nobody there. A slight quivering in the atmosphere indicated that the room was air-conditioned.

Somewhere behind the bar, where there was a door ajar, he could hear the sound of a fork, and after he had coughed once or twice to show that he was there, a young, fair-haired waiter in a white jacket, who presumably took over from the barman at slack periods, appeared with his mouth full. He spoke with a strong Scandinavian accent.

"Are you looking for somebody?"

"I have an appointment with Monsieur Beaudoin."

"You're sure it's for now?"

"At three o'clock."

A little clock, standing among the bottles, said exactly three o'clock.

"In that case, he'll be here any moment now. Take a seat."

He was wondering which armchair to choose when a man came in, hatless, balding, and with a busy look about him.

"Monsieur Jeantet, I suppose?"

"Yes."

"Come over here, will you? . . . There, now! This table will be fine."

It was in an alcove, a long way from the bar. The man sat down, crossed his legs, hitching up his trousers, and took out a gold cigarette case bearing his monogram. "Do you smoke?"

"Thank you."

Monsieur Jacques held out a lighter that matched the case, and the two men all but touched one another.

"Have I kept you waiting?"

"No. I'd just arrived."

"I preferred to meet you here rather than in my office. I suppose you can understand why?"

"Perfectly."

Beaudoin, looking ill-at-ease, was surreptitiously studying Jeantet, as if he could not make up his mind about him. They must have been about the same age and they had been born a few miles from one another. One of them was in the habit of giving orders and being listened to and, here, he was in his accustomed setting. Yet he was the one who seemed to be the more uneasy of the two, and the other's silence clearly worried him.

"May I ask why you wanted to see me?"

He was on the defensive, possibly fearing an attempt at blackmail. Or perhaps, as Gordes had thought for a moment, though in his case without really believing in the possibility, he was afraid that Jeantet was armed.

Not only was he not armed, but it was without any feeling of anger that he gazed at the man whom Jeanne went to meet every Wednesday on Rue de Berry and who, for a whole year, had paid for Pierre's keep.

He obviously led a very busy life, finding time, in spite of his work and the hundreds of people who depended on him, to lunch and dine out, to go to theaters and night clubs, to entertain in his apartment at Neuilly, to stay at Deauville and Cannes, to go shooting in the autumn, and to drive his car or take a plane as others took buses.

"Did you love her?" he said at last.

He had not prepared the question. It had just sprung from his lips, and he himself heard it as if his voice were coming from a long way off, from another world.

The waiter spared Beaudoin the embarrassment of replying.

"Would you like something to drink, Monsieur Beaudoin?"

The latter turned to Jeantet as to a guest.

"A brandy? . . . A liqueur? . . ."

"A glass of mineral water."

"For me, any kind of fruit juice."

And, when the waiter had gone:

"Was that what you wanted to ask me?"

"I don't know. . . . No . . . More than anything else, I had to see you. . . ."

Now that he had seen him, he thought he understood. Still, he went on to ask quietly, almost regretfully, because he could not help it:

"What did she say to you about me?"

"If I understand your question correctly, she refused to leave you and was anxious that you should never find out the truth. She was terrified of hurting you."

"Why?"

Beaudoin was beginning to show signs of impatience, now that he realized that Jeanne's husband was not dangerous.

"Because she'd got it into her head that she was indispensable to you."

"Did she tell you why?"

"You really want me to go into details?"

"No. I wanted to be sure that she'd talked to you about it."

"If it will help to cut short a conversation that I find disagreeable, I can assure you that there's nothing about your life or hers that I don't know."

"Would you have married her?"

"If it had been possible . . . In any case, that's nobody's business but mine. . . ."

"Did she write to you?"

"Practically every day."

Jeantet was not in the least interested to know that Jeanne had been mailing letters secretly while she was out shopping.

"I'm not talking about those letters, but about the one the police gave you."

"The police haven't given me any letter. . . . Thank you, Hans . . ."

He drank a mouthful of fruit juice. Jeantet felt no desire to touch the quarter-bottle of iced Vichy water he had been served.

"Yet she wrote a letter. . . ."

"How do you know?"

"The chambermaid saw it . . . One of the inspectors put it in his pocket. . . ."

"Massombre, the one who came to my office?"

"I don't think so. Another one. Possibly Inspector Sauvegrain."

"And the letter was for me?"

"I thought at first it was intended for me."

"And now?"

"I don't know. I'm beginning to wonder if I wasn't right after all."

"Was that what you wanted to talk to me about?"

He nodded, without much conviction.

"Is that all?"

"Didn't she tell you anything else? Was she very unhappy with me?"

Monsieur Beaudoin took a cigarette, omitting to offer one this time, looked at the clock, far away over the bar, and suddenly turned sharper, more aggressive.

"You didn't know, I suppose, that you were suffocating her with your so-called kindness? You'll forgive me if I find it hard to believe in such simplicity on your part, Monsieur Jeantet. You had to have her guilty, ashamed, and miserable, because you couldn't have borne living with a normal woman. . . ."

A wave of anger rose to his head and made him clench his fists as he sat in his armchair, facing an impassive Jeantet, who seemed to be smiling.

"What did you come here for? Did you hope I'd take pity on you and beg your forgiveness for taking your wife from you? You, you never gave her anything. You asked everything of her. Don't you understand that a human being needs something more than living day in, day out between four walls, waiting till somebody who's thinking about something else condescends to beckon to her and pat her absent-mindedly on the head?"

He broke off for a moment, his eyes full of contempt.

"Perhaps, after all, that's what you needed to be told. You aren't just a sick man. You're a kind of monster, and at this very moment you're so pleased with yourself you look positively blissful. You had to see in the flesh the man your wife went to meet every week because her hunger for life was stronger than everything else, than her pity, than . . ."

"She used the word *pity*?"

"A few minutes ago, I felt sorry I'd come. Now, I'm glad. Lately, perhaps, I was beginning to feel a certain pity for you too. . . ."

Jeantet remained impassive, and it was remarkable to see how he sat there, motionless, in an armchair that was not his own, in an unfamiliar setting, gazing at a man from whom a whole world separated him.

He asked in a calm voice:

"Have you thought about the boy?"

This was enough to fluster the other man.

"I shall go on paying for him, of course. I may not have done so this month because of my journey to the States. I shall have to ask my secretary . . ."

"I've already paid for his keep."

"Then I'll reimburse you."

"No. It isn't a question of money."

"If I understand correctly what you're getting at, it's impossible for me, as a family man . . ."

"I know. But I can."

"You mean . . . ?"

"Not right away, because the boy will have to get used to the idea . . . He will, little by little. And then, one day . . ."

Beaudoin was not sure what he ought to think. He suddenly wondered whether he hadn't made a mistake, whether he hadn't been wrong.

"You intend to adopt him?"

"Yes."

"I don't see how I can stop you."

"You can't."

"You've nothing else to tell me?"

"No. Except that Jeanne is buried at Esnandes."

"I know. I also know that you didn't go to the funeral."

"Did you?"

"No. But my case is different. Besides, I was in Boston."

"Yes . . ."

Jacques Beaudoin got up and, after a last look at Jeantet, who stayed in his armchair, went over to the bar.

"Put the drinks on my account, Hans."

"Yes, Monsieur Beaudoin."

It was over. Or almost over. For the rest, Jeantet had to wait nearly a month, for he did not want to go up to the fourth floor. He waited for Mademoiselle Couvert to come and ask for the money.

She came down on the appointed day and knocked at his door.

"I'm sorry to bother you, but we are at the thirtieth today and . . ."

"Come in, Mademoiselle Couvert. The money is waiting for you."

He had changed again since the last time, and it was beginning to worry her.

"Sit down . . ."

"But the boy will be coming back from school any minute now. . . ."

"I know. . . . It's about him that I wanted to have a word with you. Lately, in the course of our encounters on the stairs and in the street, I've begun to soften him. . . ."

"You've given him a cowboy pistol and a box of colored pencils. . . . And it's you too, isn't it, who has been buying him ice cream?"

"He already hates me less than he did. . . ."

147

"What are you trying to do?"

"Little by little, he'll understand."

"What will he understand?"

"That I'm not his enemy and that I wasn't his mother's enemy . . . That his place, one day, will be here. . . . No, don't worry, not right away . . . I'm going to leave him with you a little longer."

"What on earth are you talking about?"

"I intend to adopt him. I've talked about it to Inspector Gordes."

"And he approves?"

"He was surprised, but he finally understood and he'll help me with the formalities."

She could not believe her ears, and started breathing quickly.

"So after the mother . . ."

She looked at the walls around her as if they were those of a prison, as if the apartment were a sort of trap, a snare for human beings. . . .

"But what do you want to do with him?" she cried suddenly, feeling at her wits' end.

"And what about you? Have you forgotten that, but for me, there would be nobody to pay for his keep?"

She was beaten. A little later, she dragged herself slowly upstairs, muttering under her breath.

He shut the door behind her. He was alone again, but not for long, and, instead of sitting down in his armchair, he went over to one of his drawing boards to work at the unfinished alphabet that one day people would call Jeantet type.

In a little apartment in the Ternes district, Madame Sauvegrain, who was plump and fair-haired, with dimples in her cheeks, was putting away in a wardrobe the summer clothes that would not be needed again until the following year. Some had come back from the laundry, others from the dry cleaner's, and she looked to see that there were no buttons missing, felt automatically in the pockets.

That was how, in a pair of light-colored trousers her husband had not had occasion to wear for several weeks, she came across what must have been an envelope. It was now nothing but a piece of yellowish pulp, on which she could see there had been some writing and on which a few printed letters that had survived immersion in the washing machine could still be deciphered.

H TEL G DE A

She thought right away of the Hôtel Gardénia because, one day, when her husband had come home for lunch after making inquiries in a hotel where a woman had died, she had told him:

"You'd better change before having lunch. . . . Your clothes smell of the corpse. . . ."

There were some brown stains on the trousers, and she remembered that she had made her husband take a shower while she put out some clean clothes and underwear for him.

She wondered whether she should tell him about what she had found. In the end, she decided not to, considering that he already worried far too much about his work.

Thus Inspector Sauvegrain, who had thought of everything except that pair of trousers, never knew what had become of the letter.

Jeantet never discovered that he had been right, that Jeanne had written, after all, that it would probably have been enough to read the letter to understand.

But had he needed to do that?

Noland, 15 July 1959